A Rhapsody of Ravens and Revenge

Dynamis Security

Liliana Hart

Copyright © 2024 by Liliana Hart

All rights reserved.

Published by 7th Press
Dallas, TX 75115

All rights reserved. This book or any portion thereof may not be reproduced or used in any manner whatsoever without the express written permission of the author except for the use of brief quotations in a book review.

This is a work of fiction. Names, characters, businesses, places, events and incidents are either the products of the author's imagination or used in a fictitious manner. Any resemblance to actual persons, living or dead, or actual events is purely coincidental.

Also by Liliana Hart

JJ Graves Mystery Series

Dirty Little Secrets

A Dirty Shame

Dirty Rotten Scoundrel

Down and Dirty

Dirty Deeds

Dirty Laundry

Dirty Money

A Dirty Job

Dirty Devil

Playing Dirty

Dirty Martini

Dirty Dozen

Dirty Minds

Dirty Weekend

Dirty Looks

Addison Holmes Mystery Series

Whiskey Rebellion

Whiskey Sour

Whiskey For Breakfast

Whiskey, You're The Devil

Whiskey on the Rocks

Whiskey Tango Foxtrot

Whiskey and Gunpowder

Whiskey Lullaby

The Scarlet Chronicles

Bouncing Betty

Hand Grenade Helen

Front Line Francis

The Harley and Davidson Mystery Series

The Farmer's Slaughter

A Tisket a Casket

I Saw Mommy Killing Santa Claus

Get Your Murder Running

Deceased and Desist

Malice in Wonderland

Tequila Mockingbird

Gone With the Sin

Grime and Punishment

Blazing Rattles

A Salt and Battery

Curl Up and Dye

First Comes Death Then Comes Marriage

Box Set 1

Box Set 2

Box Set 3

The Gravediggers

The Darkest Corner

Gone to Dust

Say No More

Laurel Valley

Tribulation Pass

Redemption Road

Midnight Clear

And the Raven, never flitting, still is sitting, still is sitting
    On the pallid bust of Pallas just above my chamber door;
    And his eyes have all the seeming of a demon's that is dreaming,
    And the lamp-light o'er him streaming throws his shadow on the floor;
    And my soul from out that shadow that lies floating on the floor
    Shall be lifted—nevermore!

— Edgar Allan Poe

Chapter One

Russia

Ten Years Ago…

He decoded numbers and patterns like most people breathed, and computers had been an extension of his body since before puberty. Even stuck in an elevator shaft, with sweat dripping down his spine, his fingers flew across the keyboard of his laptop, closing in on one of the most dangerous hackers in the world. They called her the Black Lily. But to Cypher, she was as close to his equal as he'd ever found. And this game excited him like no other.

The elevator jerked to a stop and the doors slid open with a clatter, but his fingers stayed steady. The smell of dust, something dead in one of the ventilator shafts, and rusted metal burned the inside of his nostrils. The temperature was almost unbearable—his skin slicked with sweat and amplified by the heavy gray coveralls he wore.

The heating system in the old building seemed to shoot directly into the elevator shaft instead of the cavernous space where the heart-thumping techno music shook the rafters and writhing bodies danced with abandon. But he knew how to separate pain and discomfort from the job. The job came first. *Always*.

His adrenaline spiked and his blood pumped faster as the death trap below him picked up speed and took him to the fifth floor. The spinning turbine above and the jagged edges of metal gave him some concern, but he'd programmed the elevator he was on top of to go no higher than the fifth floor. The sixth floor was shut down for construction. But still…there was the sharp edge of worry that something might go wrong. But a little bit of fear was a healthy thing. It kept the mind alert and the body ready for anything.

"You okay, Cyph?" Ghost asked through the comm unit in his ear. "Your heart rate is through the roof."

Gabe Brennan was team leader for this mission. He was the oldest of all of them and had been in the game the longest. And his call sign couldn't have been more appropriate. He *was* a ghost. Because Gabe Brennan didn't exist, and no one could find him if he didn't want to be found. Not even Cypher. And that was an ability that deserved enormous respect.

"I'm fine, Mom. Just enjoying the ride to the top. And praying to God you don't have to scrape my guts out of that turbine."

"I'll pass on that job," Warlock said from his position across the street as lookout. "You had that leftover Thai for breakfast and an entire pizza for lunch. If you didn't work out like a machine you'd be seven hundred pounds."

"Jealousy doesn't become you, War," he said without heat. "It must be nice sitting across the street eating Russian donuts while we're doing real work over here."

Warlock—also known as Nathan Locke—huffed out a laugh. "It's not so bad, now that you mention it. There's a hot little brunette that just paid off the bouncer. Lord have mercy."

"If you ladies are done, we're supposed to be on a mission here," Reaper interrupted.

Cypher grinned even as sweat dripped into his eyes. Atticus Cameron's voice got softer the more irritated he became. And by the sound of it, he was *very* irritated.

"Any change in Yukov's status, Ghost?" Atticus asked.

"We're about ten minutes away from the club," Gabe answered. "He's not in any hurry. Stopped to get cigarettes. You'd never know by looking at him that he's about to buy nuclear launch codes and try to start World War III."

"A wily kind of guy, that Yukov," Atticus said. "I wish I could say the same about our ever so outgoing financial wizard. Kraus hasn't moved from the VIP lounge for the last hour and a half. His nervous tics are so obvious they're making *me* nervous. And he's about halfway through his third whiskey."

"Yukov only needs him to make sure the money is deposited in their account and then rerouted to a safer location before the Black Lily double-crosses him," Gabe said. "I'd be nervous too if I was Kraus and knew I had to go up against the Black Lily's computer skills. If Kraus fails, Yukov will put a bullet in his head right in the middle of that VIP lounge and he won't care who sees him. Yukov is invincible in this country."

"Well, that'll be fun," Atticus said. "How's it going, Cyph? Any closer to pinning her down?"

"In the last half hour she's bounced me from Paducah, Kentucky, to Amsterdam to Antarctica to Greenland. If she's half as attractive as her computer skills then I can't wait to meet her in person."

"That's assuming she'd give you the time of day to begin with," Warlock said with a snort. "Women have a tendency to run the other direction whenever they see you. You're a scary-looking dude. Your reputation precedes you."

"I'll take that as a compliment."

"Focus, Cyph," Gabe interrupted. "We've got about twenty minutes before this whole mission goes to hell. Find her."

"On it, boss. I've narrowed her down to a three-mile radius. She's in the city, just like you suspected."

"She's too greedy." Cypher could hear Gabe's smile over the comm unit—like a shark right before it bit into its prey. "She could've made this entire transaction go through from halfway across the world. But she likes to watch."

"My kind of woman," Cypher said, smirking as he closed in on the Black Lily's location. She was practically right under their nose. Now they just had to find her in the crowd.

The Black Lily had been the bane of his existence for the past four years. He'd had no idea where she'd come from. Hackers—or at least the good hackers—could recognize the work of others, and there was a hierarchy. Once certain tasks were accomplished then the hacker would move up the chain to establish his or her reputation.

He'd been ten the first time he'd hacked into the Pentagon and CIA databases. If only the world really knew what happened to John F. Kennedy, boy would the stuff hit the fan.

At twelve he'd managed to bring Vegas to a screeching halt. It was hard for casinos to operate when all their money had vanished. And hey, he'd given it back. Eventually.

At fourteen he'd been too cocky for his own good and interfered in a military operation that could have cost the lives of a lot of soldiers. He'd been lucky it had been Robert Lockwood who'd showed up on his doorstep one afternoon and not the FBI ready to drag him away in cuffs and lock him away forever on any number of charges.

Lockwood had been Assistant Deputy Director of the CIA at that point and he'd given

Cypher two choices—go to prison and never touch a computer again, or come work for the CIA.

It hadn't been as easy a choice as one might think. He'd thought of running. He had money and skills most people only dreamed of. Not to mention he didn't particularly want to be on the right side of the law. He was too good at being bad. And it paid a whole lot more.

But there'd been something about Robert Lockwood that had made him rethink his choices. He was a man who commanded respect, and he said exactly what he thought and always meant what he said.

So he'd reluctantly shaken hands with his new mentor, packed his bags, and left the life of a teenage boy behind for something bigger. But boy did he miss that punch of adrenaline at knowing he could slip in and out of any system in the world and take whatever he wanted. He tempered those needs by breaking as many rules as he could get away with and generally being a pain in everyone's behind.

The name Cypher was legendary, even twelve years after the day Robert Lockwood had found him. And still, no one had ever managed to pull off the feats he'd accomplished when he'd walked on the wrong side of the law. But the Black Lily had come close.

The disturbing thing about the Black Lily was she'd appeared out of nowhere. Which meant she was either very, very young when she'd started or she'd been lying low, biding her time in the underground community and studying her prey.

He'd been searching for her identity for the last four years—where she'd come from, what she looked like. But that information was as elusive as the woman herself. He'd set traps for her and watched time after time as she'd slipped through his fingers like grains of sand. It had become his personal mission to bring her down.

And then the opportunity had practically fallen into his lap. Sometimes luck was better for solving cases than anything else. Michel Yukov had been high priority on the CIA's watch list for almost a decade—international terrorist, broker, arms dealer, assassination attempts—pretty much any crime that could be thought of if the price was high enough from the buyer.

"Gotcha," Cypher grinned. "You're all mine, baby."

"Good job, Cyph," Gabe said. "We're about three blocks away. Don't take your eyes off our targets. Once the meet between Yukov and Kraus takes place those launch codes will be in the wind. You've got to intercept those codes."

"I'm on it," Cypher said, the salt of sweat stinging his eyes. "It's showing she's on the third floor, VIP lounge, northwest corner."

"Umm, I hate to break it to you, Cyph," Atticus said, "but I'm staring straight at the northwest corner of the VIP lounge and the only person sitting there is Kraus."

"Look harder." Frustration compounded the headache brewing behind his eyes and he built more traps, trying to see where she'd slipped by him. But the report came back the same. "She's there, Reaper. Keep looking. She'll be young. Very young. Late teens to early twenties."

"I've got the profile memorized," Atticus said. "And I'm telling you she's not here."

"Hell," he said, slamming his fist down on top of the elevator.

"One block out and closing," Gabe said through his earpiece.

"Uh, oh," Warlock said. "We've got agency interference that just walked through the front door like she owns the place. All one hundred and ten pounds of fiery redhead."

They all listened as Gabe swore under his

breath. "What is she doing here? That woman drives me crazy."

"That's exactly the reason she's here," Atticus said dryly. "You guys need to learn how to date like normal people."

"I'm going to blister her for this."

All of a sudden there was a new voice speaking through the earpiece.

"You boys are a man short for a job like this," a sultry voice said. "Kill Shot reporting for duty."

"On whose orders?" Gabe demanded. "This isn't your op. You're barely out of training. When I get my hands on you—"

"Slow down, hot stuff. Take a breath. Last time I checked Lockwood's orders outranked yours. He said to get my skinny tail here, so here I am. I caught up on the intel on the plane.

"Fine, and we'll talk about whatever it is you're not wearing later."

Cypher winced and shook his head. He could practically hear the steam shooting from Gabe's ears, but Gabe would bury the anger and move on. One day all that repressed emotion was going to blow like a bomb.

"Enough," Gabe said. "Cypher got a lock on her and says she's in the building, but she's playing with us. Keep your eyes and ears open."

The elevator doors opened again and a man and woman stepped inside. Cypher could see them through the flimsy metal ceiling panels he'd been trying to avoid since he'd climbed through them several hours before to start the prep work. The man was tattooed on every available inch of visible skin and a barbell ran through his nose and both eyebrows.

Cypher could appreciate the artistry of tattoos —his shoulders and arms were covered in them— but he had to draw the line at so many piercings in the face and writing the word *DIE* across the forehead. Even *he* knew that couldn't be good for job prospects.

The woman with him must have been his perfect match because her torso, neck, and face were similarly tattooed. She wore a black mesh shirt, short leather skirt, and black combat boots.

Weirdly enough, Cypher felt right at home at clubs like this one. He'd always had more of an edge than the others. He shifted as quietly as he could, but still the elevator ceiling creaked beneath him. The couple didn't notice as the bass thumped hard enough to rattle the walls, and his own heart was pounding along with the beat.

His legs were asleep and his laptops were strategically placed on the reinforced beams. The computers were Velcroed down, but still they jostled as the elevator came to a stop on the fourth floor. The doors opened and the couple stepped out into wall-to-wall bodies. The smell of sweat assaulted his senses along with the underlying sickly sweetness of marijuana.

"It's a good thing I don't get motion sickness," he said as the elevator once again made its way to the bottom floor.

"That's the least of your problems," Warlock said. "This building is so far past fire code that you'd burn to death before you could get out of that metal death trap and through all the bodies in there."

"As always, War, you're just like Santa Claus with your cheery goodness."

The elevator doors opened again and a laughing couple stood at the doors, ready to get on, but at the last second the girl wiggled out of his arms and spoke quickly in Russian, letting him know she'd meet him back at the bar after she found the restroom. The guy squeezed her arm and gave her a kiss before drunkenly making his way back toward the bar and another drink.

The girl hit the button for the third floor and then leaned back against the wall. She was a curvy little thing, fitting just right into a black leather skirt with silver studs that barely covered her. Leather boots came to just above her knees and her cleavage was nicely displayed in a leather bustier. Her hair was short and white blond and slicked back from a face he still hadn't gotten a look at, but if it matched her body it would be spectacular.

It was almost too late by the time the hairs on the back of his neck stood up. The elevator picked up speed and they flew right past the third floor that had been her original destination. She looked up at him through the grated ceiling and gave him a grin that made his blood run cold. She couldn't see him, but she knew he was there.

But he could sure see her. And the face did match the body. Unfortunately, it was a face he recognized. He'd know those stunning violet eyes anywhere. They'd always unnerved him, too large and serious to belong to a child. But she sure as heck wasn't a child now. She'd grown into those eyes.

The floors zipped by and his pulse scrambled as they passed the fourth, then fifth floor. She'd overridden the hold he had on the elevator to stop.

"Hell," he whispered, even as he slammed his

computers closed, hoping the information inside of them would be saved on impact.

He was going to die. An agent the government would never claim, killed in the line of duty, crushed in an elevator shaft halfway across the world.

"Cypher," Gabe commanded. "What's happening?" A man like Gabe Brennan didn't panic. He was ice.

"She's in the elevator," he said quickly. He rolled flat and used his fist to punch through the flimsy metal ceiling panels just as the elevator jerked to a stop a few feet from the spinning turbine.

He went ass over elbow into the elevator, along with his laptops and the rest of the ceiling, but he rolled to his feet quickly in case she tried to finish him off before she saw his face. His computers were toast, and that pissed him off all the more.

If it had been anyone else in this situation he would've laughed, but he wasn't finding anything funny at the moment. If everyone came out of this alive and with their jobs intact they'd be lucky.

She leaned against the corner of the elevator, out of the way of the debris, as if she hadn't a care in the world, a smirk on her full lips and her gaze buried in the tablet-like device in her hand as she issued it commands. A device that was still in the prototype phase and wasn't out on the consumer market yet. He had one very similar to it. And he wondered where she'd been hiding it because there was barely breathing room in that outfit she wore.

He took the comm unit from his ear and dropped it on the ground, crushing it beneath his heel. He'd never sacrificed the mission for anyone or anything before. But he was about to break that rule. Because he owed one man his life.

She didn't bother looking at him, and he wondered where she'd gotten the balls to stand there like the stakes were too small to mess with. He would've admired her for it if he hadn't been so furious.

"You've been out of play for too long, Cypher. You're nosing your way into someone else's game," she said in Russian. "I expected much more from someone with your reputation, but it's clear your day is over. You lose. I'll see you down to the bottom floor so you can make your way out."

She leaned forward to press the button to go back down, but he reached up and grabbed her arm. He wanted to shake some sense into her, and he couldn't remember the last time he'd been so angry he was trembling with rage. Her head came up and her mouth opened to spew something at him, but she finally got a good look at his face. And all of the color left hers.

He didn't give her a chance to work her magic on her device, but instead jerked it out of her hand and took her by the arm like a willful child. She *was* a willful child. What was she? Eighteen? Twenty? And when he saw the fear on her face he realized how little she knew about the kind of game she was playing.

He hit the *door open* button on the control panel and then pulled her into the cavernous sixth floor, quickly jamming the elevator door so no one else could use it.

Cold drafts of air blew from one side of the floor to the other. Some of the windows were missing and large sheets of plastic were tacked over them, rattling and flapping beneath the piercing wind. He welcomed the cold air as it blasted his overheated body.

"You've got about five minutes to explain to me why I should save you. You have got to be out of your mind, Evie." The angrier he got the more pronounced his Lowcountry accent. You could take the boy out of South Carolina…

She flinched at the use of her name, but straightened her shoulders and tried to jerk out of his hold. He had an even bigger urge to cover her up. She'd changed a lot since the last time he'd seen her. And he wasn't altogether comfortable with it.

Sweat glistened across her skin even though puffs of white from the cold escaped her mouth. Her pulse fluttered in her neck and he could see the fear in her expression. But she didn't back down. She'd always had more attitude than common sense. Because he was really, really pissed, and that defiant tilt of her chin was close to sending him right over the edge.

"I'm twenty years old. You're not my keeper, Cal."

"You sure as hell need one, sugar. What is your father going to say? You're not only bringing yourself down, but you're ruining the career and legacy of one of the best men I've ever known. So start explaining yourself." He let her go and then stood with his legs slightly spread and his arms crossed over his chest.

"Chill out," she said. "It's just a game. You know that better than anyone. Right, *Cypher?*"

Her lips were slicked red and she smirked at him, arching an eyebrow in challenge. His body jerked in response. She was bad, bad, bad, and for some reason that appealed to him. He was going to be in big trouble if he didn't get his act together.

"To think it was you all this time," she purred. "My biggest challenge. I've got to say, I thought the smell of victory would be sweeter."

"Yeah, congratulations, Evie. You win. You're surrounded by one of the best black ops teams in existence. I've got your computer," he said, holding it up, "and we have all the data showing that you're about to sell nuclear launch codes to one of our country's biggest enemies. So tell me again how you beat me?"

She rolled her eyes and shrugged. "It's not like the launch codes are real. I'm not an idiot. And despite what you think, I do know what my father does for a living. Saint Robert Lockwood. America's top spy. Looks like he doesn't know everything."

Tears glistened in her eyes and he wondered what happened to the little girl who'd followed him around the first time he stepped foot in the Lockwood home as a fourteen-year-old boy. She'd annoyed him to no end. Yet he'd never told her to go away. She'd been eight years old and one of the only friends he could remember having during his childhood.

He thought of Robert like a second father, but he had no clue what the relationship was like between father and daughter. The tug of sympathy in his chest surprised him. He wasn't the kind of man to show empathy or dole out forgiveness. And here he was ready to do it for a half-grown girl who deserved a better life than the one she was setting herself up for.

"You should be the last person to judge." Anger flashed in her eyes. "You know what it takes to work your way up the hierarchy. I pull this off and I'm queen."

"Are you really so naïve that you think you can double-cross a man like Yukov and get away with it? You think he doesn't have his own personal army of hackers? You've heard of Tsar Ivan, right? He's been off the grid as long as I have. Who do you think he's working for?"

Cal shook his head in frustration. "You're playing an adult's game with the common sense of a child. Yukov will hunt you down and kill you if you deliver him fake launch codes. And he will kill you painfully."

"So what am I supposed to do? If you say

someone like Tsar Ivan is working for Yukov then it looks like I'm screwed either way. Ivan might be out of the game, but I've studied his work. He's been around a long time. And he's good."

"He's not better than me," Cal said. It wasn't an empty boast.

"You'd fix this for me?" she asked, the surprise evident in her voice. "Why would you do something like that?"

"First of all, because of your father. He was more of a dad to me than my own ever was."

"Yeah, I know," she said, rolling her eyes. "All I ever heard about growing up was you. You're the son he never had and I'm the daughter he never wanted."

"Cut the crap, Evie. You know how many meals I've sat through hearing about awards you received, milestones you made, and boyfriends that would never be good enough for the daughter of Robert Lockwood? You're that man's world, and you're living in a fantasy.

"Which is the second reason I'm doing this," he said. "I remember the little girl with the curious eyes and adult brain who followed me around like a puppy. And the teenager with braces and an infectious laugh. You're doing yourself and everyone who knows you a disservice. So yes,

I'm going to fix this for you, but you're going to do it on my terms. My rules."

"Go to hell, Cal."

Her eyes flashed fire and defiance, and the heat under his skin had nothing to do with the temperature inside the room. He shook his head to clear it and his anger turned toward himself. What was wrong with him?

"My rules," he repeated. "You have ten seconds to make a decision. Then I'm going to turn you over to the team."

Her eyes bored holes into him as he counted down the seconds. He wasn't bluffing. And she wasn't budging. He was about two seconds from saying to hell with it all and throwing her over his shoulder when she nodded her head.

"Fine. Your rules."

"The Black Lily dies tonight," he said. "Every trace of her will be wiped from existence. Game over."

Her mouth dropped open in shock. "You can't do that," she argued, her voice getting louder. Her hands fisted and he wondered if she was going to take a swing at him. He couldn't blame her if she tried. "She's everything. The best part of me. You have no idea what you're doing."

"I know exactly what I'm doing to you. And

you're wrong. She's not the best part of you. She's a criminal. Evangeline Lockwood runs circles around her, and she'll always be the better of the two in my mind. You relinquish everything having to do with the Black Lily. Not even a whisper of your presence in any of the underground circles. I'll be watching."

"You're taking everything away from me. I'd almost rather die."

"That'll be your choice," he said harshly. "Or you can grow up and put your talent to use. Finish college. Do something worthwhile instead of being hell bent for your destruction and everyone else's. You think I don't understand the pull? The power that comes over you when your fingers touch the keyboard? The lust to walk on the wild side anonymously from the comfort of your bedroom? I was you. And I can tell you as sure as I'm standing here that if your father hadn't shown up on my doorstep then I wouldn't be here today. So yes, I know *exactly* what I'm doing to you. And for you."

"I don't need the lecture. I agreed to your terms."

"The lecture is free. Right now you're thinking the Black Lily is your true identity. The part of you no one knows and no one really understands.

She's more interesting and smarter. But that's nothing but a bunch of lies.

"I know Evangeline Lockwood," he insisted. "And she's not this person. She's good. And kind. She makes cookies for teenage boys who find themselves at her dinner table for Thanksgiving and Christmas, and she talks to animals when she thinks no one is listening. She's strong and smart. And *interesting*. And believe me when I tell you I can count on one hand the number of women I've met who fit that description."

Tears streamed down her cheeks, smearing the heavy eye makeup she wore. She was a pretty girl. And one day she'd be a beautiful woman for someone else to handle. Thank God. Because she had more spirit than anyone he'd ever met. She was only a little misdirected. And he had to get the hell out of this room and away from her because she was scrambling his brains. Maybe it was her eyes. They'd always haunted him.

Between the adrenaline rush and his need to take care of her—out of a sense of guilt or camaraderie he couldn't be sure—he felt himself being tangled in a web that would be hard to get out of. Her mind fascinated him. Her talent challenged him. And her body made him have thoughts he had no business having. There was only six years between them in age, but those six years seemed like a lifetime.

"I hate you for this," she finally said. "I'll do it, but I'll hate you forever."

He was almost relieved. "I can live with that. Plenty of people have hated me before."

"Then what are you waiting for? It's time for the Black Lily to die."

Chapter Two

Present Day…

Evangeline Lockwood was almost positive a person couldn't die from boredom. Because if one could, she'd surely be dead.

She woke up every morning at five thirty, showered, ate a protein bar, brushed her teeth, and dressed in whatever she pulled out of the closet. Today it happened to be a pair of overalls and a tiny white T-shirt that showed her midriff, paired with chunky white sneakers. Apparently the nineties were making a comeback. Not that she bothered with fashion much anymore.

She slapped on some moisturizer—because she was thirty and she'd started to notice the little lines at the corners of her eyes—and piled her dark blond hair on top of her head. Like clockwork, she made it out the door in time to catch the seven o'clock train into DC.

Her office building was just like any other office building. She used her badge to let herself in and rode the elevator with the same people she saw every morning at the same time. She made sure to wear her earbuds and blast Olivia Rodrigo so she didn't have to talk to anyone.

She and Kai—who also had his earbuds in—were the last two on the elevator as they got off on the twelfth floor. Evangeline gave him a wave as she made her way to the communal kitchen area and grabbed a green juice smoothie before making her way to her cubicle.

There were certainly worse jobs in life. She'd had a couple of them. She'd walked dogs in college, which turned out to be a disaster since she was allergic to dogs. And then there was the short stint as a bartender. It turned out bar owners didn't like it when you broke expensive bottles of liquor over a jerk's head. She didn't particularly like it when a jerk tried to stick his tongues down her throat, so flipping her boss the double bird and quitting had seemed like the right thing to do.

College had been a breeze. She'd graduated early and started on her master's. She'd gotten bored with it about halfway through, not believing what the Ivy League school had to offer was really the most challenging curriculum out there. She could've done the work in her sleep. She'd gotten the job offer from Imaginex the week after she'd stopped going to classes. The job offer had helped cushion the blow when she told her father she'd quit grad school.

The money was good, but creating the software for video games wasn't her passion. Her passion lay in another area entirely, and she was pretty sure reputable companies didn't want what she had to offer anywhere near their businesses.

She didn't have the creativity some of her coworkers had. She could do the technical side of the job faster and better than anyone else, but she didn't have the same vision. She wasn't an artist or a storyteller. And that was fine. But after six years of doing the same thing day in and day out—moving from one project to the next—she was starting to wonder if it was time to start looking for something new.

A wadded-up piece of paper flew over the top of her cubicle and landed on her desk, followed by a loud *psst*. Dark eyes peered at her over the partition that divided her and Joseph Wong's desks.

"You up for a get-together tonight?" he asked.

"Keep it quiet, but we're going to test out the demo for *Aviator* and order pizza. We're going to play on the big screen at Jay's house. Bring dessert if you're coming."

"I've got plans tonight," she lied. "But thanks for the invite."

"Cool. You're missing out though." And with that Joseph went to the cubicle next to hers to extend the invitation to the next colleague.

Keeping to herself had become par for the course for the last six years. She didn't socialize with the people at work. Didn't hang out in the break room or go for drinks at five o'clock. There was no point befriending people who would never know the *real* her. And if they knew the real her they wouldn't want to be around her anyway. It would more than likely bother most people to know she could have their entire life history with a few strokes of the keyboard—from finances to emails to doctor's reports. Everything was attainable online.

Her skills as a hacker had only improved as she'd gotten older. She knew how closely Cal watched her movements and monitored her time online. How he searched for her through the underground channels, looking for signs of her old self. The Black Lily had died that day, just like she'd promised. But someone else had been born—someone she could be proud of.

Evangeline spent just as much time monitoring Cal as he did her, looking for that telltale sign that he knew what she'd been up to for the last ten years. But it never came. She'd gone to a great deal of trouble to keep her new identity a secret. And it gave her pride a nice boost to know she'd finally surpassed the master.

Not that she could ever tell him. Cal didn't say things he didn't mean, and the second he found out she was breaking his "rules" he'd turn her in. She was under his thumb for the rest of her life—at least on the surface. And he could never be trusted again. She'd grown up with him, seen him as a friend and someone she didn't have to hide her intelligence from like she did with other kids.

That's what had hurt the most about the way he'd treated her. Yes, the choices she'd made were the wrong ones. And she was grateful her eyes had been opened to the danger she'd involved herself in. Cal was the one person she'd thought had really understood her. He was her equal. All of her fanciful girlish dreams of happily-ever-afters had lived and died with Calvin Cruz. He'd killed every dream she'd had—of respecting her skill and thoughts of spending her life with him.

Of course he'd never seen her that way. The only reason he'd done what he had and "saved" her was because of her father. Not because he cared about her in any way. But Cal had taught her a valuable lesson. Love was a foolish emotion. The mind and how one used it was all that was important in the chess game of life.

Her game had changed over the last ten years. Cal had been right about one thing. She was headed for destruction if she'd kept on the same path of her youth—playing the dangerous games of one-upmanship within the hacker community. But she was smarter than that. If she wanted her cake and to eat it too she had to minimize the risk without minimizing the rush of adrenaline she longed for. Not an easy task.

So she went to her boring job and lived her boring life. And she took tastes of freedom in small doses when she could.

By the time the clock on her computer screen said four o'clock she was ready to climb the walls of her cubicle. By the time five o'clock hit she grabbed her backpack and dared anyone to try and stop her on the way out.

Summer was in full swing and the heat weighed heavily across her shoulders as she stepped outside and breathed in the exhaust fumes and hot pavement. Cars sat bumper to bumper, ebbing and flowing as the stoplights dictated, and someone down the street sat on their horn as a group of pedestrians blocked traffic.

Ahh, she loved the city. No one paid attention. No one cared. You could slip into the shadows without anyone knowing, and you could stand in the middle of a crowded street and be completely anonymous.

The muted sound of a phone ringing had her digging around in her backpack until she found what she was looking for. One look at the caller ID and she almost didn't answer it. Their conversations had been the same for the last several years. And she didn't have the energy for it today. She needed to soak up what was left of the sunlight and get rid of the pounding headache that her cubicle tended to bless her with on a daily basis.

"Hello, Daddy," she answered.

"Evie, come for dinner tonight. Carla made that roast chicken thing you like. And she says there's chocolate cake for dessert."

"Carla doesn't make dessert unless company is coming. Who else will be there?"

She crossed the street at the crosswalk and contemplated grabbing a newspaper from an outdoor stand. A lot of interesting information could be gleaned from what was reported in the papers. And by interesting information she meant the truth. She never knew where her next job was going to come from. She dug for some cash in the front pocket of her overalls and paid the guy, grabbing a paper and shoving it in her backpack.

"Dr. and Mrs. Reinhold and a couple of private contractors from Dynicorp. It's very casual."

"And I'm sure the private contractors are both single and meet your requirements for a suitable husband?"

"I have no idea what you're talking about, Evangeline. I'm a busy man, and I take offense that my own daughter thinks of me that way."

"Uh-huh," she said. "I'm sure you're crushed. You always say the truth hurts."

Her father had made it his mission since her mother's death to get her settled down. He thought he was being subtle, assigning her bodyguards when she was required to play hostess for him. Or sending former agents or analysts to her home if she needed something done around the house. She'd almost laughed to the point of pain when he'd sent one of them to help her build a fire pit in her backyard. She'd have had it done in a couple of hours if it weren't for the "helpful" interference of a man who thought he could do it better.

"Little girl, that's no way to talk to your father."

"I'm going to have to pass tonight. I've got plans."

"What kind of plans?" he barked.

Her father wasn't used to being told no. He'd been the boss for too long. Fortunately she'd had lots of practice over the years.

"You never have plans," he said, not giving her a chance to answer. "You're going to rot away in that house alone. Go out and have some fun. Make friends. Your isolationism is getting past the point of ridiculous."

"When did you turn into a nosy old woman instead of my father?" She smiled when he *hmmphed* on the other end of the line.

"I beg your pardon? I am *not* a nosy old woman. I'm the ex-Director of the CIA."

"Ahh, there he is," she chuckled. "Why don't we talk about your hobbies, Daddy? Like maybe you should get some because being a matchmaker doesn't really suit you. You're quite bad at it."

"You've become entirely too cheeky since you

turned thirty. Which is well past the age of settling down and starting a family."

"And the old woman is back," she said with a sigh. "Maybe you should be tested for multiple personalities. I've got to tell you though, if you start wearing one of those lacy scarves on your head like Aunt Tilda I'm going to call in a professional."

"I've never looked good in lace," he said dryly.

She laughed and said, "Enjoy your chicken dinner and chocolate cake. I love you." She hung up before he could bring up her lack of a social life again. She lived her life exactly the way she wanted to.

The crosswalk sign turned white and she went against the flow of pedestrians to the other side of the street, heading away from the snarl of traffic. The smell of red sauce from the little Italian place on the corner made her mouth water, and she thought briefly about stopping in for dinner. But she immediately felt the guilt of turning down her father's invitation and walked on by. She had salad stuff in her fridge at home. That was punishment enough.

The sun sat like an orange ball of flames just above the row of buildings on the opposite site of the street. It was hot enough to melt the soles of her shoes to the sidewalk, and she could feel tendrils of hair curling at the base of her neck. It was the miserable kind of heat—the kind that made it hard to draw in a breath and sucked the energy right out of the soul.

She stopped for a moment to dig her sunglasses out of her bag and remembered she'd left them on her desk. She swore and slung her bag over her shoulder and a man jostled her as he passed by, not bothering to say excuse me. Her head snapped up to say something sarcastic to him but the words stuck in her throat.

"Oh, God," she said as a silent prayer.

A silver car jumped the curb of the sidewalk, not ten feet in front of her, sending a couple of outdoor restaurant tables flying. The glass vases that had sat at the center of each table shattered against the pavement, and it was nothing but good luck that no one was seated outside.

Time slowed and her eyes widened in horror as the car door swung open. All she could think was that it was just like a movie. An arm lifted and the dull sheen of the black gun glinted in the sunlight. His hands were nice. Like an artist. Or a piano player. With long fingers and a light smattering of dark hair on the back of the hand. She was close enough to see the gleam of a gold wedding band just before his finger moved to the trigger.

She was the daughter of the former Director of the CIA. She'd trained and taken classes her entire life just in case. Her father always told her it never hurt to be prepared. Her instincts kicked in and she dropped to the ground, rolling for whatever cover she could find. It happened to be one of the overturned tables and she prayed no stray bullets would end up coming her direction.

The gunfire sounded like it came from a cannon it was so close, and she watched as his hand jerked—*one, two, three* times—as he squeezed the trigger.

The man who'd jostled her fell straight to his knees. He was so close she could almost touch him, could've reached out and touched the bottom of his shoe. She pulled her knees into her body so she was a smaller target, but there was nothing more she could do to protect herself.

The shooter's hands dropped to his sides, silver cufflinks gleaming at his wrists. Time froze and the silence after the last bullet was deafening. No one moved and the sounds of the city disappeared into a void she couldn't explain. There was a split second of time where nothing existed.

And then reality whooshed back with perfect

clarity. The man toppled to his side and his head hit the sidewalk with a terrible crack. People screamed and car horns blared and everything went into motion once again. But there was nothing she could do for the dead man beside her.

She looked away, trying to find anything else to see other than the empty-eyed stare of a stranger. Instead she looked into the face of the man who'd pulled the trigger. And he was smiling. Not at her—he hadn't even noticed she was there. But he smiled, a slash of cruelty over what would otherwise be handsome features.

Tires squealed and a car door slammed. And then the man was gone. The entire event had taken only seconds. Seconds for one man to take the life of another. People were still screaming and the blood still rushed in her ears, but she could hear the sirens in the distance.

Her knee throbbed and her teeth chattered uncontrollably. A limp and lifeless hand lay inches from her, but she had to make sure. She reached out and touched his wrist, but there was no pulse beneath the skin. And then she noticed the blood.

It pooled beneath his prone body, so dark it was almost black, creeping closer and closer to where she lay. She glanced at his face one more time and recognition registered. Her skin went cold and clammy and her breathing shallowed. Darkness crept in at the corners of her vision, but she was determined to not give in to blessed escape. It would leave her vulnerable and weak, and that wasn't how her father had raised her.

The enormity of what had just happened hit her. Senator Myron Biddle was dead. And she'd be replaying his murder in her mind for the rest of her life.

Chapter Three

"No," Cal Cruz said. He knew better than to say it, but he couldn't help himself. It was a gut reaction.

"I beg your pardon?" Atticus Cameron raised a dark eyebrow and the jagged scar along his jaw turned white.

Cal recognized the tone of Atticus's voice. He wasn't happy. Not that Cal could really blame him. There weren't very many people in the world who had the guts to tell Atticus Cameron no. Only people who didn't know any better. Or idiots. Cal was pretty sure he fell into the second category.

"I apologize," Cal said quickly. "You caught me off guard. I meant to say 'No, sir'."

"I'm going to pretend you didn't just say that so we can move on without anyone getting fired or killed."

"I'm okay with getting fired if it means not having to take this job."

"Then we'll take that option off the table and go with door number two."

Cal was pretty sure Atticus was kidding. Though Atticus liked to keep things close to the vest. They'd been friends a long time, and worked together longer than they'd been friends. And still Cal wasn't 100 percent sure that Atticus wouldn't slit his throat in a second if push came to shove.

"What's the problem, Cal?" Atticus folded his hands on the top of the file in front of him. "You're like a son to Robert Lockwood. Why wouldn't you want to take this mission? It doesn't make any sense."

"I can see how it wouldn't make sense to you. But it makes perfect sense to me. I'm going to have to respectfully decline. I'm due for some vacation time. I think now is a good time to take it."

"All vacation time has to be approved, and I can promise you that I'll crush any dreams of vacation for the foreseeable future if you don't take this mission. You're the only available agent I have for the job. Max is in Israel, and Nate and Eden are in Guatemala. Jade is leading a team of agents in Rio, I've got a black ops team in Syria, and a couple of deep cover agents in Moscow. I'm tapped out. And there's no way in hell I'd trust a junior agent with Robert Lockwood's daughter. You're up to bat."

"You know I hate doing fieldwork. My job has always been behind the scenes."

"I know you hate it, but that doesn't mean you're not trained for it. And you still haven't explained why you're whining like a little girl about a job that should be one of the easiest paychecks you've ever earned. All you've got to do is go to Florida and protect her until the killer is found."

"That could be years, Atticus." And he sure couldn't live in close quarters with Evangeline Lockwood for years. Not even for a few minutes. That was a disaster waiting to happen.

They'd seen each other only a handful of times in the past ten years and hadn't spoken one word. She hadn't been kidding when she'd told him she'd hate him forever. But darned if that hatred had kept her out of his dreams.

Cal had stopped visiting the Lockwood home for holidays, and he'd gotten in the habit of meeting Robert at restaurants, the gym, sporting events, or on the golf course—though his golf game had never been all that good.

"I want to know what is going on here, Cal. I tell you that Robert calls me in a panic to say that Evangeline is in danger and needs protection and you blow it off like it's no big deal. You're not a jerk. At least not most of the time. So that means something is going on."

"I can't believe you fell for it," Cal said, shaking his head in disbelief. "You of all people should know what he's been up to over the past several years. Robert has hired bodyguards for Evie ever since that assassination attempt he had a few years before he retired. He's an overprotective father. And he's been a meddling overprotective father ever since she hit twenty-five and showed no signs of settling down into a serious relationship. Have you noticed that every bodyguard he's ever hired has been single and between the ages of thirty and thirty-five? And that most of them have a military background, good education, and no shady family history?"

Atticus's lips twitched in what might have resembled a smile. "I noticed. But he's not concerned about people getting to him through his daughter this time. He's concerned because she witnessed the murder of Senator Biddle. Not only witnessed the murder, but she got a good look at the person who shot him."

"Have there been any leads on the murder?"

Cal knew there hadn't been, but it was best to let Atticus think he was in the dark. He also knew she'd given a description to the sketch artist at the FBI, and between the artist's skill and the advanced technology the FBI had access to, she'd come up with a pretty remarkable likeness. She'd been questioned extensively and sent home, and they'd promised to keep her name and the connection out of the public.

Cal had kept a close eye on Evangeline ever since he'd gotten her out of that nightclub in Russia ten years before. He knew everything about her—from how often she checked her email to the one lover she'd briefly had. He'd felt responsible for her the past ten years, to make sure she was living a life that her father could be proud of. But what he'd done was become responsible for killing the spirit that had made her one of the most formidable opponents he'd ever gone up against.

She'd changed her appearance. Gone was the

flash and spark of the young woman who'd consumed his thoughts for months—no years—after that one encounter. She had a respectable job and lived a boring life. But she was safe. And that's all that really mattered.

Atticus pushed the file across the table, but Cal didn't pick it up. "A lot of speculation is all they have at this point. Biddle was Chairman for the Committee on Armed Services, and no telling what he was working on or who he was working with."

"I can find out easy enough. It's been a while since I hacked into the Department of Defense. I don't want my skills to get rusty."

"Yeah, what's it been? A whole week?" The corner of his mouth tilted slightly. That was equivalent to a full-blown laugh for Atticus.

"Hey," Cal said. "This is why you pay me the big bucks. It's always good to know who our competitors are in this business."

"And I appreciate it," Atticus said deadpan. "As long as you don't get caught and destroy my company and send me and all of the agents under my command to prison. I'd prefer not to have to kill you."

"That's the second time you've threatened to kill me today. You're getting more violent in your old age. Have a little faith, man. I'm the best."

Atticus shook his head. "Someone always comes along who's better. It's important to remember that. Otherwise you end up dead. Besides, to hear Gabe Brennan talk, the hacker kid he has working for him can run circles around anyone."

He shrugged. "Nah, I've already checked him out and made his life interesting. He's got some years to go before he one-ups me, so you can relax. He goes by the name Dragon, which is just stupid if you ask me."

"I'm sure he'd love your input."

Cal grinned unrepentantly and said, "I've already given it to him in my own special way. He's good. Very good. But a little rough around the edges still. Gabe was smart to recruit him. He's definitely someone we want working for the good guys."

"Thanks for the office gossip." Atticus grabbed a bottle of water from the little refrigerator built into his desk and tossed it to Cal before grabbing another for himself. "Maybe you could read the file and stop changing the subject. What are you, twelve?"

Cal unscrewed the cap and relaxed farther

back into the chair, not touching the file. "Come on, Reaper. What is this really about? We both know what Robert's agenda is here. He hasn't had any luck pairing her off with one of his chosen bodyguards so he's expanding his breeding pool a little. Though he'd probably blow a gasket if he knew you were planning on sending me. I don't think Robert considers me son-in law material. Hell, even Julie's parents threatened to disown her if she married me. They knew I was trouble the minute they met me. And it turns out they were right."

Time had lessened the pain of Julie's death, though it had hardened Cal in ways he'd never thought possible. Settling down wasn't for everyone. Especially not someone who lived the life he had while in the CIA. He still wasn't sure how he'd survived those years. How any of them had survived. And if he was honest with himself he never should have settled down with Julie. He hadn't been ready for marriage. And the long hours, travel, and secrets had put a burden on their union from the start.

"You know, Cyph, of all the agents I've worked with, you're the only one I've never been able to understand what the hell was going on inside your head. For someone with more brains in the tip of his fingers than most people will ever hope to have, you manage to underestimate and undervalue yourself. And when you underestimate and undervalue yourself, everyone else starts to believe it's true."

"Thanks for the advice, Pollyanna, but I'm just telling you the truth. I promise you that I would be the last choice Robert would pick to guard Evie. I'm not marriage material. He told me so after Julie died. He said men in our professions are better off being alone because we don't bring anything but loneliness and heartbreak to the people who love us. And damned if I've ever forgotten those words."

"The part of me that buried my wife would agree with you," Atticus said. "But despite the hand that was dealt to me and Jane and our daughter, I would never trade a second of the life we shared together. That's how rare and special it was. I appreciate that more than ever now.

"It's about finding the woman that makes you a better man—a better agent—and complements your personality in ways you never imagined. The *right* woman will make you wonder how the hell you ever survived thirty-six years without her."

Cal shook his head, the obvious pain and grief of Atticus's face hard to look at. "What you and Jane had was special. She understood you in ways that even your own team didn't. I wasn't sure such a thing was possible. What you had was a one in a million shot. For the rest of us…let's just say I won't be calling a bookie to place a bet on lightning striking twice. Besides, I'd rather be hung up by my toenails than to go through all that again. Which is why I don't want to be the sacrificial lamb to Robert's matchmaking attempts."

"This time I don't think matchmaking is at the forefront of Lockwood's agenda, Cyph. Someone trashed Evangeline's townhome last night."

Cal took a long drink of water and tried to get his racing heart under control. "Was she hurt?"

"Fortunately, she worked late and missed her train. She ended up staying overnight at Robert's home. She had clothes there, so she went to work like any normal day, and then pulled up at her house a little before six o'clock this evening."

Cal calculated the time difference. "That's barely two hours ago. You work fast."

"Nobody messes with Robert Lockwood's daughter," Atticus said. "He's out for blood. Evangeline had a bad feeling the minute she opened her garage door. She told the responding officers something just felt off, so she decided to park street side instead of pulling in where she might get trapped before calling the police."

"She's got good instincts," Cal said. "Robert raised her to be cautious."

"With good reason. Her place wasn't just trashed. It was gutted. Everything was destroyed. Shoes, clothes, pictures, dishes—"

Cal didn't move a muscle. His skin went cold and his grip on the arm of the chair was so tight he was surprised it didn't snap off in his hand. He had to check the urge to make sure she was safe for his own peace of mind. Emotional reactions never solved any problems.

He'd learned to separate the emotion from logic and reason. He'd been accused on more than one occasion of being as much of a machine as the computers he worked on, but in his mind it was the only way to survive the atrocities he'd seen over the twenty years he'd spent in the bowels of covert ops.

"And none of the neighbors heard or saw anything? She's got houses on both sides and neighbors across the street. It's a safe neighborhood."

Cal finally reached for the file Atticus had pushed toward him. There was no turning back now. Despite his vow to stay out of her life, he knew it wasn't a vow he had any intention of keeping. She was going to be pissed. But her safety came first.

"None of the door-to-doors came up with unusual cars or strangers in the area. The police have virtually nothing to go on. Despite the damage that was done to her house, it was a very well-executed plan. She'd be dead if she hadn't missed her train."

Cal's head snapped up at that bit of information. "What are you leaving out?"

Atticus's mouth tightened and his eyes went stone cold. "When the police entered the residence there was blood everywhere. The neighbor's cat was slaughtered and a message left on the wall in blood. Whoever murdered Senator Biddle knows Evangeline can identify him. The media posted the artist's drawing along with her name as the eyewitness. No one knows who leaked the information."

"Of course not." Cal's blood boiled. He'd never had much use for the media, but deliberately risking someone's life for the sake of a story wouldn't be tolerated. If Atticus didn't find out where the source came from then he sure as hell would.

"What did the message say?" Cal asked.

"It said, 'You're next.' There were no prints, fibers, or hairs left on scene. As soon as Robert was notified, local PD was pulled out and the FBI was brought in. Their crime scene people were thorough. Take a look at the computer rendering of Senator Biddle's shooter."

Cal flipped through the file until he saw the sketch. "You're kidding me. That's Victor Taber. That scar on his forehead is unmistakable." He looked at the image a little closer just to be sure, but it was Taber. Eyes, black and soulless, stared back at him, and a jagged scar in the shape of a sickle was just over his left eye. *Hell*.

Cal closed the file and stood up, already heading for the door. Time was of the essence. He wasn't sure he'd ever experienced such heart-pounding fear as he had when he realized who was after Evangeline.

"Who's watching Evie now? God, Atticus, Taber could put a bullet through her head before anyone knew there was a threat."

"Relax, I've got men on her," Atticus assured him. "And Robert is with her. They're travelling to that giant pink compound in Florida. She'll be safe and well guarded until you get there."

"And then what? She's got a professional hit man out for her. One of the best any of us has ever seen. Has Taber ever missed an intended target?"

He squared off against Atticus and folded his arms across his chest, waiting for an answer. Atticus didn't move from behind his desk. He leaned back in his chair and picked up a pen, rolling it between his fingers.

"Tell me, Reaper. Has Taber ever missed a target?"

"You know he hasn't," Atticus finally said. "He's the best there is. But so are we. I don't hire anyone less than the best."

"What does Evangeline know?"

"Nothing about Taber and the level of danger she's in. As far as she's concerned it's a vendetta against her as a witness. For that matter, Lockwood doesn't know about Taber either. Taber's professional work started a couple of years after Robert retired from the CIA, so he's an unknown entity."

"She's going to resist, you know," Cal said. "She's headstrong and stubborn on her best days. The last thing she's going to want is my protection. *Especially* my protection. She hates my guts."

"Are you saying you can't handle her?" Atticus asked, his brow quirked curiously.

Cal blew out a breath. "That's not what I'm

saying. I can handle her just fine. She's just not going to like it."

"As long as she stays alive she doesn't have to like it. And you can make her love you again. You've been known to pull out the charm when you want. Must be that South Carolina drawl that makes women turn to putty in your hands."

Atticus went back to whatever he'd been working on before their meeting and Cal knew he'd been dismissed. He headed toward the door, running through the argument he and Evie were sure to have the moment she realized he was going to be her bodyguard, and wondering how he was going to keep her safe. Taber was batting a thousand in assassination attempts.

"Oh, and Cyph," Atticus said. "Maybe someday you'll fill me in on what really happened on that mission in Russia. Evangeline didn't always hate you."

Cal didn't turn back. Atticus always saw more than a person intended—could infer more from a look or a hesitation than most people could get from a full written confession. It was one of his gifts.

Instead Cal kept walking, the decision already made to make things right between him and Evie. Because there was no way he could be that close to her and keep his feelings to himself. He'd fallen hard for her, and she'd haunted his dreams ever since. He'd married Julie in the hopes of forgetting Evangeline. It hadn't worked, and he'd always feel guilty for pulling an innocent woman into a game she'd never agreed to.

But Evangeline was his future. And it was time to put the past where it belonged.

Chapter Four

Robert Lockwood considered himself a patient man. He'd headed the CIA for a decade, overseen countless ops, and dealt with politicians without bloodshed. Surely that made him qualified enough to deal with his daughter.

"Evangeline," he said. "You're overreacting. Take a deep breath and sit down. This isn't at all how I taught you to respond during a high-tension situation. Emotions cloud logic and have no place during a mission."

"I'm overreacting?" she said, stopping her pacing to stare at him in disbelief. "You take all of my choices away like an errant child and put me in lockdown in another state with a contingency of bodyguards who all happen to be eligible bachelors and *I'm* overreacting?"

Only a lifetime of training kept him from wincing at the bite in her voice. Saying she was angry was an understatement. Energy practically crackled around her. Her hair had always been as reddish gold as a sunrise, but he couldn't remember the last time he'd seen it down. She always wore it pulled back. Even in Florida in the middle of the summer she was as unassuming as ever in a pair of baggy lounge pants and an old T-shirt. She'd spent the last ten years trying to hide away so no one noticed her, never making an effort to cultivate relationships or move out of her comfort zone. He worried about her a great deal. She hadn't always been that way. Something had changed in her a decade before and he had no idea what it was.

He never thought he'd miss the wild and adventurous and sometimes rebellious child she'd been. But it had been a long time since he'd seen a glimpse of that girl. There was a part of him that was glad to see her anger.

Whatever had happened to change her a decade before, it had only intensified after her mother's death. Robert had built a career on noticing things, and he was even more determined to get Evangeline to enjoy life. He knew better than anyone how precious and short it was.

He'd lost a good woman and a lot of men under his command during his almost seven decades on earth. And he'd be damned if he'd give up just because his daughter was throwing a temper tantrum.

"Daddy, are you listening to me? You've got that look on your face you use with politicians where you pretend to listen but you're really thinking of all the other things you need to do."

He laughed for the first time since he'd heard the news about the threat made to her. She was his heart and soul, and he'd do whatever it took to keep her safe. He wasn't always the best at showing his love, but he did it the only way he knew how. To try and make sure she was safe and secure. In his mind, that was the most anyone could ever ask for.

"You look just like your mother when you get angry. Have I ever told you that?"

She growled at him and he held back another chuckle. If she was anything like her mother in temperament she'd be throwing things at his head before too long. God, he missed that woman. She'd been his partner in every sense of the word, and there'd been a void in his life ever since her death.

"You forgot to mention that there's a maniac

after you who doesn't particularly want you to be able to be a witness when he's caught and this thing goes to trial."

"Daddy—"

"Don't you *Daddy* me, Evangeline Elizabeth Lockwood. There's a difference in being independent and just plain foolish. And this time you're being foolish."

"I can take care of myself, and I can hire my own bodyguards if I feel I need them. The police and the FBI are watching my house. I'll be perfectly safe staying there. This guy killed a senator and destroyed my home in broad daylight. He's making stupid choices. There's no way he can keep doing what he does and not get caught. I'll be just fine at home."

"Uh-huh. And I'm sure it won't bother you at all to stare at the broken things you've worked so hard for and the blood on the walls." He shrugged his shoulders and gave her a sarcastic look. "Heck, the ambiance might do you some good. What was I thinking? Let's call a cab and get you back home."

She rolled her eyes and he knew he had her. Children were predictable creatures after all. At least to a certain extent.

"How long am I supposed to stay here?" she

asked, finally dropping down onto the couch across from him. "I have a job. I have responsibilities. I can't just take off indefinitely while the investigation continues. The last I checked they were no closer to finding the identity of Biddle's killer than they've been from the beginning."

He took a sip from the bottle of water in his hand and thought carefully how to best answer. "We've got some added help from superior sources," he finally said. "Sometimes jobs like these call for the best. And I just happen to be in the business of knowing who's the best. Trust me. We'll know who killed Senator Biddle very soon."

"If you've got everything worked out then there's no point in me wasting my time and the money you're spending on hired goons."

"I'm not sure your new bodyguard would appreciate being called a goon."

Robert's lips twitched. Cal Cruz had been called a lot of things in his thirty-six years, but he was pretty sure that goon wasn't one of them.

"All I'm asking is that you give it a week," he said reasonably. "Think of it as a vacation for my peace of mind. Myron Biddle had his fingers in some pretty interesting pies. Believe me when I tell you that the list is long for those who probably wanted him dead. And the people on that list are very good at killing. I'd prefer my only daughter wasn't added to the body count."

"I'll give it a week," she said. "But you and I both know that living hidden in fear is no way of living at all."

"I dislike it intensely when you use my own words against me."

She grinned and he saw the little girl he remembered—the precocious child with the brain of an adult who'd given him every gray hair on his head. She'd been a handful, and he'd not always known the best way to deal with her. But he'd enjoyed every minute of it. Or almost every minute.

She'd once decoded the intelligence reports from the operatives he had placed in Iran. It had taken her about five minutes to read what had taken him almost two hours. And he'd gotten a tongue-lashing from his wife that still sent shivers down his spine once she found out he'd let a six-year-old girl decode an entire report—most of which wasn't at all suitable for a child.

It was a good memory. And he was getting maudlin in his old age. Maybe he *was* becoming an old woman.

The hairs on the back of his neck prickled and the atmosphere in the room changed. Despite the fact there'd been no noise to alert his presence, Robert knew they weren't alone anymore. Cal was good, and he felt a swell of pride to know that he'd been the one to train him.

"If you keep zoning out I'm not going to help you host that party at the end of the month," she said.

"I'm not zoning out. I'm compartmentalizing all the different things I need to do today."

"So you're ignoring me? That makes me feel much better, thank you."

"I hate that shirt you're wearing," he said, just to be contrary. "You could fit Barnum and Bailey under there."

"Men your age shouldn't wear shorts," she countered. "You've got legs like a chicken."

He snorted out a laugh and then made the transition in conversation abruptly. There was no point in delaying the inevitable.

"Since you're in such a good mood let's talk about your bodyguard."

"Really, Daddy, you're getting ridiculous with your matchmaking attempts," Evangeline said. "It's obvious to everyone involved."

She propped her bare feet up on the coffee table and crossed her ankles. "Who is it this time? An ex-Navy SEAL? An Army Ranger? I hope it's someone with a sense of humor. You've sent some real duds lately. I've barely been able to stay awake once they start talking about themselves."

His lips pinched and he steepled his hands in front of him. "Now, really. You're being ridiculous, Evangeline."

"You always get very proper whenever you get called out. Have you ever noticed that? Of course you have," she said, before he could answer. "You were the Director of the CIA. I'm sure you're familiar with all of your weaknesses."

"Little girl, a little respect please. I've always said that smart mouth of yours is going to end you up in hot water one day."

"Sorry, Daddy. I have no idea where I get that from," she said, cheekily. "I've told you before I have no desire to get married and have children. No matter how badly you'd like to see that. I've got everything I want in my life."

"That's perfect. Because this time I'm not trying to use my matchmaking skills."

She arched a brow in surprise. "So you're admitting that's what you've been doing all this time with the personal bodyguards?"

Her father smiled and shrugged unrepentantly. "You're my only child. I just want you to be happy. I also want you to be safe. Which is why your protection comes above all else in this case. Besides, I'm out of single men who fit the profile. You've broken all their hearts."

She chuckled and crossed her arms over her chest, snuggling down a little farther into the couch. Maybe she could use a vacation. She hadn't stayed at the beach house since before her mother's death. If you could call a three-story pink monstrosity a beach house.

He'd bought the house for her mother the week after she'd been diagnosed with breast cancer. Her father was a tough man—unbending on his best days and something not worth mentioning on his worst days. But he'd been a softy when it came to his wife. She'd been happy at the beach house for almost three years longer than the doctors had given her to live.

Evangeline cleared her throat and pushed away the memory. "So if you're out of poor saps you can marry off your daughter to, who are you left with? Attila the Hun?"

"Not too far off," a voice said from the doorway behind her.

Her blood chilled and her head snapped

toward the Lowcountry drawl she hadn't heard in years. Surely her eyes deceived her. She blinked once—then once more—but his image didn't disappear.

Calvin Cruz in the flesh looked better than he had any right to. Better than she remembered. And her memory was pretty good. He'd always been the kind of man people noticed. It wasn't his looks so much as the way he carried himself. He had an aura about him that screamed danger.

His hair was black as sin and he wore it longer than he had ten years before when he'd been on active missions. Crystalline blue eyes stared at her mockingly, inherited from his Swedish mother, and his skin was swarthy, inherited from his Mexican father. Dark brows winged over his eyes, and he hadn't shaved in a few days so he had a thick growth of beard.

She didn't know if she was normal when it came to what a woman found attractive about a man. But she'd always been captivated by Cal's shoulders. The breadth and strength of them, and how nicely they filled out the black T-shirt he wore. The black ink of tattoos showed below his sleeves, more than he'd had the last time she'd seen him. He wore loose linen pants the color of wheat and she wondered if he was carrying a weapon. She wasn't sure it mattered if he was armed. If she saw Cal Cruz walking toward her in an alley, she'd turn around and run the other direction. He was dangerous with a capital *D*.

"Like what you see, sugar?" he asked, arching a brow.

Her cheeks flushed red and she looked at her father accusingly, but Robert was suddenly very interested in his water bottle.

"Oh, no," she said, shaking her head. "No, no, no. This is my worst nightmare."

"Come on, Evie," Cal said, coming farther into the room. "It'll be just like when we were kids."

His voice sent a shiver down her spine. How could one man have such power over her? She hated that about herself. She knew she was smart. Could make her own decisions and live an independent life without the help of anyone. Yet one man had controlled her entire destiny for a good portion of her adult life—a man she couldn't trust far enough to throw him. And still his presence affected her like no other man's ever had.

Her pulse fluttered in her throat. No matter how much she'd told herself she hated him, it was still Cal she saw in her dreams. A childhood crush that had never faded.

"Go away, Cal."

"It's the middle of summer and we're at the beach," he said. "Let your hair down for a while. Stop being so uptight. You used to be fun."

"And you used to not be a jerk. I guess time changes us all."

She closed her eyes for a moment and counted to ten, focusing on the sound of the ocean. The sliding glass doors were open and if she made a run for it she could have the sand between her toes in just a few seconds.

"Well then," Robert said, getting to his feet. "It looks like three's a crowd. I'll leave you two to get acclimated. I've got a plane to catch."

"Oh, no," Evangeline said, standing. "You're not going anywhere until you explain what the hell is going on."

"I told you, Evie. You need a bodyguard and I'm out of eligible bachelors. That leaves Cal. You agreed to take precautions for the week. Don't go back on your word now."

She narrowed her eyes at him, but it was a wasted effort because he'd already turned toward Cal.

"Son, you always did have a way of making women want to claw your eyes out."

"It's a gift," Cal said, grinning.

Evangeline could count the number of times she'd wanted to do violence to a person on one hand, and she was pretty sure they all involved Cal.

There were very few people in the world who knew the real Calvin Cruz. Maybe not even her come to think of it. He was brilliant, no doubt, and that brilliance was only one of the aspects she'd found fascinating about him over the years. The layers of Cal had always intrigued her. And it was obvious to anyone who knew him well that he covered a whole world of hurt with smart remarks and general rudeness if it suited him.

He'd never cared one bit about being anyone other than himself, and he never made apologies for his behavior. People either loved Cal or they hated him. There was no in-between.

"You might as well take him back with you, Daddy. There's no way I'm going to let Cal be my bodyguard. You know his attention span won't last the week. He'll be playing poker with the staff and fleecing them out of all their money after two days."

"Still bitter about that are we, Evie?"

She turned to face him, putting her hands on her hips. "I was twelve, you moron. And no, I'm not still bitter. Some of us learn to grow up. Want to take a guess who in this room hasn't?"

"Not really," he said with a shrug. "If by 'grow up' you mean turn into a boring spinster who doesn't know how to have fun I think I'll pass."

"You made me what I am," she said, and then she remembered her father was standing there and pinched her mouth shut before she said too much. "Get out of my house." She was surprised by how even her voice was. Because on the inside she was screaming. "If you're not out in the next ten seconds I'm going to shove my fist down your throat and jerk your cold, worthless heart right out of your body. And then I'm going to feed it to a shark along with the rest of your corpse."

Cal arched a brow and gave her an insufferable smile. "You've given that a lot of thought, Evie. Kind of disturbing if you ask me. I don't remember you being so violent. I wonder where all this pent-up aggression is coming from. Have you thought of seeing a counselor?"

A sound came out of her mouth that was somewhere between a gasp and a shriek. "I'm going to kill you. Murder you in your sleep. And no jury would convict me."

Good grief, she had to get a hold of herself. He was turning her into a shrew. The way to deal with Cal was to outsmart him. He thrived off emotional reactions, and she was giving him exactly what he wanted.

She took a deep breath and tried to smile, though she wasn't sure she was successful in her attempt. "You're right, Cal. I apologize. I'm completely overreacting. I think it's because Daddy's been pressuring me to settle down by throwing men into my path every chance he gets. My reaction is just reflex now."

The look in his eye was calculating as he tried to figure out her angle.

"You make me sound like a tyrant trying to sell his daughter to the highest bidder, Evangeline." Robert stared her down, his lips pursed. "I find that highly insulting."

"Your speech is getting proper again," she said, narrowing her eyes at him. His lips pinched even tighter together and he gave her a look that would've sent any number of his agents running in the opposite direction.

He was really still a very attractive man for someone in the latter half of his sixties. He stood military straight, his shoulders broad and his body still in good shape from years of training. His hair was thick and had been completely silver since she was a child. It was a shame he hadn't found a woman to keep him occupied so he'd stay out of her business.

"You're pushing your luck, Evangeline."

"No, Dad. I'm being serious." She shrugged and then crossed her arms over her chest. "Maybe you're right. Maybe it's time I took your advice and settled down. And you're hand-picking these men, so there must be something good about them. I figure one is just as good as the next. You've always loved Cal like a son anyway, so maybe we should just see where this goes."

The color drained from her father's face and he went completely still. She would've burst out laughing if it wouldn't have completely ruined her plan. But when she turned and looked at Cal any humor she saw in the situation dried up immediately. She recognized that look. It meant trouble.

"Now, Evangeline," Robert sputtered. His eyes cut back and forth between her and Cal, gauging the potential fallout. Just like always.

"It's okay, Daddy. I'm sure Cal knew exactly what he was getting himself into when he agreed to take this job. It's not like you've been subtle about your attempts. Now if you two don't mind, I think I'm going to lie out by the pool for a couple of hours. The idea of a vacation sounds nice now that you put the idea in my head," she told her father.

She'd taken two steps toward the door when Cal stopped her and said, "Just hang tight a minute, Evie. You and I need to go over the ground rules. This isn't just a vacation. You're going to take every precaution while you're here."

"You do love your rules, don't you, Cal?"

"Rules tend to keep girls out of trouble."

"Must be nice to make the rules and never have to follow them."

The corner of his mouth kicked up and the blue of his eyes deepened until they were almost navy. "It has its advantages."

"Am I missing something?" her father asked, looking back and forth between the two of them.

"Robert, I think it's time you left us alone to talk this out. You've set this in motion, but it's time to let us take it from here. Obviously, Evie and I have a great deal to work out. Like the fact that we're going to be sticking together like glue until this guy is caught. Atticus has added security in locations unknown to me, but they're not on the property so it's just you and me, kid."

"Get real, Cal. We can't be together every second of every day."

"Sure we can, sugar. I'll scrub your back in the

shower. By the way, I sleep on the left side of the bed."

This time it was her mouth that dropped open in surprise. The look Cal gave her was so hot she wondered how she didn't combust into flames where she stood. Heat rushed to her cheeks and things she hadn't allowed herself to feel since she was a teenager overwhelmed her. It was not a good time for her hormones to awaken. Cal had always been at the center of her fantasies. Until he'd killed them. It was important to remember why she'd stopped loving him.

"Now wait just a minute, Cal," her father said. His cheeks flushed with anger.

"No interference, Robert," Cal interrupted. "That was your promise when I took the job. You're the one who's been meddling in Evie's life, trying to get her to settle down. I'm just answering the call. You've done your part. Now it's up to the two of us."

"You're supposed to be protecting her, not seducing her. I know your reputation better than anyone, son."

"I will protect her. With my life if I have to. The seduction is just an added bonus." He grinned unapologetically and she started to worry that Cal was going too far. Her father looked ready to commit murder.

She'd never seen Cal face down her father before. Come to think of it, she wasn't sure she'd ever seen anyone face down her father. He was the boss. Larger than life. And he was no one to mess with.

"I've treated you like a son for most of your life and this is how you repay me?"

"You once told me that family never had to repay anything. You just do things because it's family."

"I'm getting tired of the two of you remembering my words of wisdom for once. And that doesn't negate the fact that you're talking about my daughter. She's not someone to dally with."

"She's standing right here and she can speak for herself," Evangeline said, irritated with both of them now. "I feel like you're about to start bartering cheese wheels and cattle for my hand in marriage. And if that's the case, then I'm going to have to shoot both of you. Cal and I don't even like each other, so I don't think this is going to be an issue."

"I like you just fine, sugar. You're the one who knows how to hold a grudge." Cal grinned. "But in all seriousness, you're not treating this situation the way you should. The man who's after you is dangerous, and I'm not going to risk your life because you don't want your privacy invaded.

"You've been a father to me, Robert," Cal said, turning to the older man. "But you set this in motion. It's time to step back and let it play out. You know I won't hurt her. But I'm also not going to stand here and let her manipulate me into letting her call the shots. And if you'd stop and think like the intelligence officer you once were and not the father you are then you'd see that as plain as I do. My first priority is to protect her. My second priority is to get her to stop being so hardheaded and realize that we can work better together than apart. Maybe that's within a personal relationship or maybe not. But it's something we'll have to figure out for ourselves."

Her eyebrows rose in surprise. She wasn't expecting something so—mature to come out of Cal's mouth. Not that she was going to give him the time of day. She certainly did know how to hold a grudge. He'd been right about that. And despite Cal's talk about personal relationships to her father, there was the little issue of trust to deal with.

What was more surprising than anything was her father nodding his head in agreement. He turned to her and said, "Cal stays. You can't fire him. Only I can do that. Do what he says when it comes to your safety. If he gets out of line with the other let me know."

Then he turned back to Cal and gave him a warning. "If you break her heart you're a dead man. I don't have time to hide any bodies with my schedule the way it is, and honestly I just don't want to deal with Atticus. But I'll do it if you force my hand. Atticus wasn't someone I liked messing with when he was one of my agents, and I want to mess with him even less now. He's a mean son of a gun when he wants to be. I think he learned that from me."

With nothing more than a quick wave goodbye, he exited the room and left them alone. The front door closed behind him, and the silence was palpable.

Evangeline felt the temper she tried so hard to control bubbling to the surface, and her hands fisted at her sides until her nails bit into her palms. The last time she'd felt this much anger and lack of control was the day Cal had taken everything important away from her.

As if reading her mind he said, "So what do you say, Evie? Do you still hate me?"

Chapter Five

Cal knew he was walking a fine line, but he couldn't seem to help himself. There was something about Evangeline that made him want to keep pushing, to argue with her just for the sake of controversy. Because the rush he got from pitting his wits against hers was better than any of the dangerous missions he'd been on.

He'd kept close tabs on her over the years, so he was prepared to see her again in the flesh. *Thought* he was prepared to see her again. She sure wasn't a girl of twenty anymore. The baggy clothes, messy bun, and no makeup didn't hide her like she'd wanted.

"Seriously?" she asked. "You're asking if I still hate you after the little stunt you just pulled? You must be out of your mind."

He winked at her and went to close the sliding glass door, testing the locking mechanism just to be safe. And then he pulled the curtains.

All the entry and exit points in the house made him want to pack her up and get her on the next plane to South Carolina to one of his safe houses, but Cal knew a monster like Victor Taber would find them no matter where they were. There was no reason to take the chance of other innocent civilians getting hurt. It was better to stay put and make his own rules.

The beach house was a security nightmare from his standpoint. The front of the house was gated by a ten-foot fence that matched the pink stucco. But the back of the house was completely open so the view of the ocean wasn't obstructed. It was a private beach. But that wouldn't matter if someone wanted to get to Evangeline bad enough. They might as well have been advertising for the bad guys to come get them.

"Sugar, I've never been more clear in my thinking. You placed the bet. I'm calling your bluff."

He closed the blinds on all the other windows and then brushed against her as he passed by. She didn't step out of his way, and he swore he could hear her heart pounding from where he stood.

"I have no idea what you're talking about, Cal." Her voice was barely a whisper.

He continued into the kitchen and she followed behind him. "You know exactly what I'm talking about, Evie. Neither of us are young and naïve. It's been ten years. That's long enough. We're too old to play games anymore and it's time to move forward."

"What if I don't want to move forward, Cal? You can tell yourself whatever you want to feel better, but the fact of the matter is that you purposely set out to take everything from me. You blackmailed me. Forced me to give up the only thing I've ever really loved. And why? Because I was getting too good? Closing in on your heels? I guess it wouldn't look good in the underground community for the legendary Cypher to get overtaken by a twenty-year-old girl."

He was silent while he checked the kitchen. It was surprisingly large and comfortable—white granite countertops and tall cabinets that the housekeepers probably hated, accented by splashes of bright colors and natural light.

An entire wall was windows and another set of French doors that looked out onto the front gardens. French doors were a thief's dream and this pink elephant of a house had six of them. What had Lockwood been thinking of buying this place?

There were no blinds to cover the windows, so he made a mental note to put a couple of extra weapons in the kitchen, just in case. The good news about the windows was that the ten-foot privacy fence and the location of the kitchen made it a more secluded area. They wouldn't have to worry about Taber getting off a long shot from the grounds. There wasn't a place he could hide. He'd have to move in up close and personal.

"I didn't take anything from you," he finally said. "I gave you a chance to grow up without disgracing yourself and your family. And the fact that you can't see that makes you narrow minded and ungrateful in my opinion."

"I don't remember asking for your opinion. And I'm more than happy to admit that I wasn't in the right. I *know* I wasn't. It was stupid and done more for kicks than anything. To prove that Robert Lockwood's daughter could do something like that and get away with it. It was an incredible high."

"I know what you mean," he said. She stood near the doorway, looking like she was ready to flee. "I could see it in your eyes. The thrill of the adrenaline rush—driving you to take chances—to up the stakes and make the high even better. You needed someone to make you stop. You never could've done it on your own. Your pride wouldn't let you."

He wanted to put her at ease so he went to the refrigerator and looked inside, settling on cold cuts and cheese to make sandwiches. "Want something to eat?" he asked.

"Stop changing the subject, Cal."

"Suit yourself. I make a great sandwich."

"Bully for you."

He grinned and got the bread out of the bread box. "You know what else I saw that night?" He left everything on the counter and closed the distance between them, testing her to see if she'd back away from him.

She didn't.

"What?" She looked up at him warily as he drew closer, until he stood only inches from her.

"I saw a woman that knew what it was to want." She started to take a step back but he took her arms in his grasp and kept her still. "She was misguided and too stubborn for her own good, but at the core was a woman who knew she'd met her match. Don't think I didn't see it for what it was."

Evie licked her lips nervously. "That's some ego you have there, Cal."

"Thank you, sugar. It's well deserved. Just like I know you have one that matches. I'm going to get real, because it's time the two of us stopped playing games. I'd been chasing the Black Lily for years before I found out your identity. I loved your mind before I ever saw your face. And after I got over the initial shock, I felt stupid for not putting it together beforehand. You're a rare jewel, Evie. And I knew it before you decided on a life of crime. For ten years I've watched and wanted you, the brains and the beauty, all while knowing you hated me."

"Uh-huh." She placed her hands on top of his arms, preparing to push him back, but he tightened his grip and brought her even closer. She gasped and her eyes widened as she looked up at him.

"We've known each other most of my life and you've never given me a second's notice. You were either in your computers or with my father. So I can say with assurance that you never gave me a second's notice."

He ignored her and kept talking, knowing the uphill battle that was set before him. "And when I found out it was you it was like being hit in the face with a two-by-four. I've been taken off guard two times in my life. The first was when I was fourteen and your father knocked on my door. The second was when you looked up at me through that elevator grate. You can't tell me it wasn't the same for you. When you realized I'd trapped you it sparked something inside of you." He leaned in closer until his lips were right at her ear. "An edge of fear?" he whispered. "A sense of danger? A challenge?"

"What are you trying to prove?" she asked. "That you're better than me? That you win? Haven't you already humiliated me enough?"

"You've got it all wrong, sugar." He felt her shiver. "I set you free. You've had ten years to grow up. To learn how to control that wild streak of yours. I know because you and I are the same. If your father hadn't caught me I'd either be dead or in jail. Your fate would've been similar. Now you've got to make the choice to come back to what you love on the right terms. On your terms."

He let the phrase soak in. What she loved.

She'd loved *him* once upon a time. A childhood crush. But no matter how he labeled it, she'd cared for him and he for her. They shared a past. Maybe they could share a future. If she didn't let pride get in the way.

She laughed, but there was no humor in it. "You mean your terms?" Her fingers tightened on his biceps as if she were going to push him away. But she didn't. "Just like that, I'm supposed to jump back in after ten years and be grateful because you said so." She scoffed derisively. "Yeah, sounds like it's on my terms."

"I'm willing to negotiate the terms," he said, his gaze narrowing. "The power was always in your hands. All you had to do was decide to use it. But for the right reasons. For the right agenda. That's something I learned the hard way. Just because you *can* doesn't mean you *should*. And your level of conscience and maturity needed a chance to catch up with each other."

"Everyone thinks their own agenda is the right one. It's why wars are fought and elections are won. Just because you fight for it doesn't make it right for everyone."

"Now you're just being stubborn, sugar. You know the difference between right and wrong the same as I do. A lot of good people would have died if you'd stayed on the path you were on. You're not a sociopath. Which leads me to the conclusion that you just didn't have the foresight to see how many lives your choices would be affecting. Your mind might work faster than most people's, but at the heart of it you were still a twenty-year-old kid who was only thinking about herself.

"You could have gotten my entire team captured that night. We would have been tortured and killed. If you'd turned those launch codes over a whole lot of people would have died."

She rolled her eyes. "I told you then. They weren't the real launch codes."

"You're not stupid, Evie. If you and Yukov had met face-to-face, no matter what your intentions with the launch codes, he would have owned you. That's if he didn't slit your throat first for trying to betray him. But Yukov is perverse that way. If he'd decided to let you live you'd have become Tsar Ivan's successor. No one on this side of the ocean would have ever seen or heard of you again."

"Yeah," she said. "So you said. I learned my lesson. I'm stuck here, just like you wanted. I'm doing a job I hate and staying off everyone's radar. You made the rules and I followed them. You won. Congratulations."

"Your life is never a game," Cal said intensely, his gaze boring into hers. "It's too precious. But you have a chance now that you have some distance and perspective behind you to play for the good guys. Now's as good of a time as any to get back in."

"Oh, gee," she said, fluttering her eyelashes. "The great and powerful Calvin Cruz is giving me permission to sit at my little computer and work magic against evil. How generous and thoughtful of him."

He shrugged. "I'm giving you the choice to take back what you keep saying I stole from you. The only thing I know for certain is that I've waited ten years to kiss you."

Cal moved in slowly, giving her the opportunity to push him away. But she stood there defiantly, daring him. He leaned in closer. Her eyes had turned a deep, dark amethyst and her pupils were large. She held on to him as if he were her lifeline.

The pleasure of not kissing her was driving him insane. He couldn't imagine what actually putting his lips over hers would be like.

It was heaven.

It was pure torture.

And he knew with that one touch that he was in deep trouble.

"Evie," he whispered.

"This is so stupid," she said. "I'm still mad at you."

"I know, sugar. But this has been a long time coming. It would've happened eventually if circumstances had been different. The other stuff will work itself out."

Evangeline was determined to put a stop to the madness. She'd made a lot of mistakes in her life. She wasn't afraid to admit it. And she'd spent a lot of years trying to make up for those mistakes the best way she knew how. Despite what Cal might think, she did have remorse over her actions. And she'd spent the last ten years in repentance, paying her dues to a society that would never care.

But as far as mistakes went, kissing Cal had to be one of the biggest.

It was every fantasy she'd ever had come to life—better than her dreams. Cal had been her first crush. Her first love. Her first heartbreak.

And though she'd dated and tried to find a partner for life, no one had ever measured up to Cal. She realized now that as right as his lips felt against hers, not even Cal could fill the hole in her heart. There was too much baggage and hurt between them.

"Evie," he said, whispering against her lips. "Stop thinking so hard. Just enjoy the moment."

She opened her mouth to say something witty, but he kissed her again and all thought left her head. She felt the panic bubble up inside of her when he stripped off her shirt.

He made a strangled sound and stared at the purple lace bra she wore. "This is the type of underwear you wear under those ugly baggy clothes?"

She tried to keep her voice light. "I have to get my kicks from somewhere."

"I should've known you couldn't repress the wild child completely," he said.

It was like cold water had been thrown on her. Her lungs tightened and it was hard to draw a breath. She couldn't do this. She hated Cal almost as much as she loved him. She'd not only made promises to Cal that day ten years ago. She'd made promises to herself.

She accepted her punishment for the crimes

she'd committed. Despite her feelings for Cal, he'd been right. She wasn't the type of person who could kill on a whim. Who could sit back while others suffered. And she'd spent the last decade keeping her head down, doing her work, and quietly helping as many people as she could. It was her penance. And penance and pleasure didn't go together.

Whatever this insanity was with Cal had to stop. She knew the kind of man he was. The job mattered more than anything. Ten years ago the job had mattered more than a young woman's childhood dreams being crushed when the man she loved looked at her with cruelty and disappointment.

And despite the want she now saw in his eyes, it was the job that mattered. It just so happened that *she* was the job. Which made it easy for him to succeed in his mission and conquer and claim her at the same time. Convenient.

"Stop," she said, pushing against him.

The panic was squeezing her now, a vice that constricted her air and her thoughts until only fear survived.

"What's wrong?" Cal asked, taking a step back and immediately looking for threats.

"We can't do this," she said. "I won't let you

do this. I'm not another mission for you to add to your win column. I stand by my promise I made to you and myself. I'll do what's right. What's just. And I'll protect the people I love. And though I'd prefer not to be held captive in my own house, and I would choose anyone else to be here but you, I understand the necessity and I don't want to worry my father. And I would like to live to testify against the man who committed murder.

"But there are boundaries. And we'll both do the jobs in front of us. Nothing more, nothing less. And when it's over we'll go our separate ways. No matter how right you were back then," she said, hating the tears in her voice. "You killed something inside me that day. Something that was innocent and pure."

She found whatever courage was still left inside of her and straightened her shoulders, staring him down with defiance. "I wanted you then. The way a woman wants a man. And I loved you then. Only you were too ignorant to see it. You can make me want you again. That's easy enough to see. But you won't make me love you again. That was a once-in-a-lifetime opportunity that you ignored. Do your job. Complete the mission. But leave me alone."

She jumped as "Master of Puppets" played

loudly from Cal's phone. They stood staring at each other as the music played, and she wished she could read his thoughts. His face was blank and gave away nothing.

The song kept playing until he broke their silence and said, "It's Atticus. The house will be swarming with agents if I don't answer."

"Then answer," she replied.

She grabbed her shirt and put it back on, covering herself as quickly as she could. She hadn't been lying when she'd told him he could make her want him again. The girlish dreams of marriage and children with Cal were just that—childish. In her heart she knew she still loved him, but she couldn't trust him. Would never be able to trust him. She was nothing more than a pawn to him. Something he wanted to control. And a guy like Cal, once he came out the victor in the game he was playing, he'd move on to the next challenge. He'd conquered the Black Lily. But he'd never conquer Evangeline Lockwood.

Her determination must've shown on her face because Cal gave her a strange look as he answered the phone.

"Cruz," he said.

She needed to escape and time to think.

As if reading her mind, he took her by the

arm before she could leave. "Like glue, Evie," he said. "Don't disappear."

She jerked out of his grasp and slipped out of the kitchen, heading upstairs to her suite. She'd just dodged the biggest bullet of her life. Now she only had to make sure she didn't put herself in the line of fire again.

Chapter Six

Cal was in deep trouble. And if he could reach his hands through the phone and wring Atticus's neck, he would have. Because this was all his fault.

That kiss would be etched into his memory forever. He could still taste her. Her words still shocked him. She'd loved him. Not a child's love, but a woman's. She'd wanted him. And he'd destroyed those childish dreams in an instant.

He couldn't and didn't have regrets. He'd do it again in an instant because he knew as sure as he was standing there that she was alive because of him. She might not love him anymore, but she was alive. He could make her love him again. *Would* make her love him again. If it was the last thing he did.

They'd been playing cat and mouse for too long. It was time for both of them to come to terms with the fact that they were meant for each other. Maybe God did have a sense of humor, because no two people belonged together—fit together—were made for each other—like he and Evangeline. He just had to convince her to agree with him.

He had a lot of regrets over the way he'd handled things ten years before. He'd damaged her pride and treated her like a child. But he still couldn't think of an alternative solution, even after all this time. He'd done what he had to protect her. And that meant more to him than her hating or not hating him. And how could she kiss him like she had if she really hated him?

What he really missed was the chase. He'd spent four years of his life searching for the Black Lily. And she'd outmaneuvered him at every turn. Except for that last time. He not only missed her as a person—they'd practically grown up together—but he missed pitting his skills against hers. There was no one else out there like her who had a combination of that level of skill and daring.

And then there was the chemistry. He blew out a frustrated breath. If Atticus hadn't interrupted them Cal didn't know what would have happened between him and Evangeline. Though he had a pretty good idea.

He wanted her the way a man wanted a woman—but not just any woman—the woman who had been made for him. There was no doubt about that. But what he wanted most was for her to trust him again. He wanted her heart. And he wanted her love. He was thirty-six years old. He was well past the point of quick and meaningless flings. He didn't want an empty relationship. He wanted someone to challenge his mind. Someone to fill the void of loneliness. And Evangeline was the only person he'd ever met who could do both.

"Cyph, are you listening to me?" Atticus asked.

"Not really," he answered. "This place is a security nightmare. What about the agents you've got on this assignment? Have they reported in?"

"If you'd been listening you would have an answer to that question. There's been no sighting of Taber in the area, and you guys are secure for the moment. You've got a weak spot on the northwest corner of the house. Beachside. No one can get in position to see from that angle, so we'll put a boat in the water so you've got eyes in that direction. Should be in place by tomorrow morning at the latest."

"What about Taber? Any sightings?"

"Not a sighting. More of a calling card. The head design engineer of AeroNaut was murdered about an hour ago in Dallas. Almost exactly the same way as Biddle. Car pulled up in the middle of the day, the window rolled down, and three shots were fired. He used a silencer this time because the streets were more crowded with pedestrians. No one got a look at his face, and he was gone and around the block before anyone could get a plate number. But the vehicle was described as a silver Mercedes, similar to the vehicle he used in DC. That's consistent with Taber's MO.

"He likes to kill in style," Atticus continued. "He studies his target thoroughly, spends a couple of weeks doing recon, following them from place to place. Ninety-nine percent of people are comfortable in their habits. They take the same roads to and from work. They stop at the same gas stations. The same few restaurants. He knows what time of day and where the hit will be most efficient. He knows what businesses have exterior cameras and where the city has cameras planted.

He has an escape route. And a plan B and C if that doesn't work out. Men like Taber don't stress under pressure. If he wasn't a psychopath, he'd have made a hell of an agent."

"Comforting thought," Cal said.

"It is what it is," Atticus said, unfazed. "Taber will be making his way toward you. You might have a few days at best if he's got other hits on his list. And from the intel we've received, we think he does."

Cal put the phone on speaker and then set it on the counter so he could go back to making a sandwich.

"You said he tapped the design engineer of AeroNaut?" Cal asked, piling a piece of bread high with thinly sliced meat. "If I recall, there was a buyout a few years ago with a new owner. He shifted their business strategies pretty drastically and pissed off a lot of shareholders. Last I checked they're doing a lot of government contracts now."

"They've got about 60 percent of the pie as far as military aircraft are concerned," Atticus confirmed. "Their last government contract was worth billions."

Cal made a mental note. "Ahh, well people have died for a lot less than that. Money is always worth digging into a little more. Who's the new head honcho at AeroNaut?"

"Well, it was John Amir," Atticus said.

"Was?" Cal asked.

"Yeah, he's dead. I'll send you the file. I've still got intel coming in from my sources, but it doesn't look like it's a coincidence. Go ahead and start probing into any connections between Senator Biddle and Amir. The sooner we cut the head off the snake the sooner we can get Taber off Evangeline's back. Whoever Taber hits next will be connected. Whoever has hired him is cleaning up loose ends."

Cal rinsed his knife off and stuck it in the dishwasher and then put everything else away. He stood over the sink, looking out across the water, and took a bite of sandwich. The waves were calm and the sun bright overhead, but he'd grown up on the water. There was a slight chop to the waves. Rain would be coming before too long.

"If I remember right—" Cal said, irritated that the weather was going to wreak havoc with his security detail.

"And you always do," Atticus said.

"—Taber doesn't take a job for less than seven figures. The higher the profile of the target, the higher the price tag. And he's just killed two very high-profile targets. Those kills are two big paydays." His words were slow and thoughtful, his drawl more pronounced. "But here's the problem. Whoever hired Taber wouldn't shell out money like that for Evangeline. She was a witness, and Taber is responsible for his own anonymity. It's part of his contract. Which means he's coming after Evangeline on his own dime. His ability to become invisible is what makes him so effective at his job. And there's only been one other time where a witness was able to identify him to the level that Evangeline can, and that was almost two decades ago."

Atticus sighed. "Taber's been in the game a long time. Longer than I have. And I remember what happened to the last witness."

"Yeah, me too," Cal said. "They found pieces of him across twelve square miles. Medical examiner said he'd been alive while he was being dismembered."

"Then you understand why I sent you to protect Evangeline," Atticus said. "All we can do is hope that Taber has other contracts to fulfill before he comes for you so we have more time to track him down. Nate and Eden got back from Guatemala yesterday. I'm giving them a day to sleep and then I'll put them in the field to apply some pressure to Taber. I want him to feel us breathing down the back of his neck."

"You don't think that will send him underground?" Cal asked.

"Not as long as Evangeline is alive. He's going to be gunning after her no matter the cost. And because she's Lockwood's daughter he's going to see it as a personal challenge. Just don't let him get the drop on you."

Cal snorted. "Thanks for the pep talk. I feel much better now."

"We're all working on this, Cyph. As soon as any agents are free I'm sending them to you. Lockwood means a lot to all of us."

Cal felt the anger start in his gut and work its way up, so he could feel the flush of rage in his neck and face. His jaw was clenched so tight he was surprised his teeth didn't crack.

"I'm not doing this for Lockwood," he said. "Evie is the one whose life is in danger. She's the one that matters."

"Like that is it?" Atticus asked.

Cal didn't hesitate. "Yes, it's like that."

"That didn't take long. You haven't even been there a day."

"It's been twenty years in the making," Cal said. "Evie's life is not a game. I'll do whatever it takes. At all costs. And if I decide that she can't be protected here we'll disappear off the face of the earth. No negotiations."

"Settle down, Cyph. We all want Evangeline safe. My name and reputation mean something in this business, and I won't settle for anything but success on any mission. You should know that better than anyone. But I need you to put aside emotion and think like an agent. We have an opportunity to take Taber out. We need to be smart in how we do it. You're right about Taber hunting Evangeline until he can silence her. And you know as well as I do that Evangeline isn't going to let you take her underground to hide for the rest of her life. From what Robert's told me about her, she'd likely slice your throat in your sleep. We have a chance to bring Taber in."

"Are you kidding me? You want to use Evie as bait?" Cal asked, his blood running cold. "I'm not going to risk her life by putting her in Taber's path needlessly. You know what he did to that last witness. He was sending a message. It wasn't three shots to the chest like his normal targets. He wanted to make sure that no one would even *think* about testifying against him. That witness died a horrific death. I can't even entertain the idea that something like that might happen to Evie. Not to mention Robert will kill us all if you dangle his baby girl like a piece of raw meat in front of a tiger."

"It was Robert's idea," Atticus said. "He was briefed in the car after he left the house, and he contacted me immediately. That's why I called you."

Cal's hand fisted, crushing what was left of his sandwich, and he tossed it in the sink in disgust. This was what he hated about the spy game. The mission was the most important thing. It was more important than people and possessions and family. And obviously it was more important than an only child.

He'd been raised in the game, so he knew it better than anyone. And he'd worked for Robert Lockwood for the majority of his career. He'd seen Lockwood compartmentalize so he could make the hard decisions—sometimes there was no other choice. But he never would have imagined he'd put Evangeline on the sacrificial altar. That meant that absolutely everyone was expendable.

The air went out of his chest. Robert Lockwood had been his hero. And now he didn't know what to think. If anything, it intensified his anger.

"What the hell, Atticus?" he asked. "This isn't what we do. Or who we are. Our jobs were to complete the mission, but we never sacrificed the innocent. We always found another way. So if that's your plan you can take my resignation and shove it. Evangeline and I will disappear before you hang up the phone. To hell with Robert if that's his way of thinking."

"You'd turn on him just like that?" Atticus asked, his voice sharp. "After everything he's done for you?"

"I'd turn on him in a second," Cal said fiercely. "She's his own daughter."

"It just so happens I'm on your side. And that's exactly what I told Robert. He is who he is. That's why he was named the Director of the CIA. Just because Evangeline is his daughter doesn't mean he can't see the big picture. It didn't take long for him to figure out that we're dealing with something Senator Biddle was working on with the Defense Committee. We could be talking billions of dollars at stake and countless lives depending on what's up for grabs. And you know as well as I do that Lockwood would never sacrifice the good of the whole for one person. Not even if that person is his daughter. Lockwood is from the old school of thinking."

"Cut the crap, Atticus. What happened to Jane was a tragedy, but you can't tell me if she were still alive you wouldn't move heaven and earth to keep her safe. You'd do the same for your daughter. You'd lay waste to whoever got in your way."

"Out of line, Cyph," Atticus said, his voice harsh.

Cal slammed his fist down on the counter and dropped his forehead against the kitchen cabinet next to the sink.

"I'm sorry, Reaper. I didn't mean it that way. I'm pissed. And a lot disappointed in a man I thought of as my father."

Cal deliberately slowed his breathing to get control of the emotions rioting through him. Emotions got you killed. And it had been a long time—ten years in fact—since he'd let his emotions get the better of him while on a job.

Guilt ate at him about what he said to Atticus. His wife and daughter had been collateral damage a couple of years before when gunmen had opened fire in retaliation to an op that had been leaked from an inside American government source. His wife, Jane, had been pronounced dead at the scene. And Anna, his daughter, had died twice on the operating table as they did surgery to repair the damage from the three bullets that had ravaged her small body. Atticus still didn't know where the leak had come from, but Cal knew he was looking with vengeance in mind.

"I'm sorry, Reap." Sorrow etched in his voice. "I really am."

"Forget it," Atticus said. "I already told Lockwood to stand down and that we'd do this my way. I call the shots for Dynamis. Not Robert Lockwood. And we're solvent enough where we could still survive without the contracts he gets us on occasion. I never cared much for politics. It's why I left the CIA."

Cal winced with regret. He should have known Atticus would do the right thing. He always did. Cal trusted him with his life. He felt like even more of a jerk.

"I know," Cal said. "So what do you want us to do?"

"What you do best. Find the connection between Senator Biddle and Amir, find out who hired Taber to kill them and see if anyone else is a possible target. And keep Evangeline alive."

Cal laughed dryly. "Just another day at the office."

"I've got local agents positioned around the area, and Nate and Eden can forgo sleep if you need them in an emergency. Otherwise look for them in a couple of days. And Cyph, don't get so wrapped up in the woman that you can't see the weapon pointed in your direction."

"Yeah," Cal said with a sigh. He disconnected the phone and went to find Evangeline. It was time they had a talk.

Chapter Seven

The house was unusually quiet. Lockwood kept a small staff on the property, but they'd all been sent away on paid vacation.

He moved through the rooms with his weapon drawn out of habit, checking windows and doors once again before heading upstairs and confronting Evie. It always gave him a bit of a surprise to walk through the private rooms and see pictures of himself mixed in with the ones of the Lockwood family. He'd always had a lot of respect for Nadine Lockwood. She hadn't batted an eye when Robert had brought him home the first time. They'd been living in DC at the time, on Dupont Circle.

He'd gone from street rat to upper crust overnight. But he'd never quite fit into their world. He'd kept his nose clean where his hacking had been concerned, but he'd found other ways to rebel, to show them that he didn't belong at dinner parties and glad-handing with politicians.

He'd graduated high school before his sixteenth birthday and had gotten his undergrad by nineteen. No one wanted a sixteen-year-old at their college parties, so he'd learned to find other ways of entertaining himself. He'd discovered his love for weights and exercise about the same time he'd discovered that there was something to be said for older college girls and their experience.

When he wasn't working for Robert he was partying and drinking in the underground, adding to his tattoos, or finding a warm bed to hone his skills. He was a perfectionist at heart and liked to do everything well. The only rules Nadine had laid out for him were that he was to respect Robert's position at the CIA, he wasn't to get in trouble with the law, and under no circumstances was he to be a bad influence on Evangeline. Those had been guidelines he'd been able to work with.

He stopped and picked up a photo from Robert's desk, his mouth quirking at the picture of the four of them on the shore in Palm Beach. Nadine had insisted they all wear white so she could get a proper photo, but the tide coming in had been stronger than they'd anticipated and a wave coming onto the shore had swept them all off their feet. They'd been drenched and sandy, and the look of incredulity on Nadine's face that nature would interfere with her family photo was worth the price. The rest of them had laughed until tears poured down their faces.

It was a good memory. One of many he had of the Lockwoods. They'd made him part of their family, despite his determination to keep his distance and bide his time until he could leave when he was eighteen. But he hadn't left. He'd been drawn into Lockwood's game of cat and mouse. Which made it even harder to accept that he'd so casually toss Evie to the wolves.

He set the photo back on the desk and headed up the stairs. The sun shone through the high windows and glared off white walls, tables and furniture. He always found it funny that the multi-million-dollar homes in this area were always decorated the same. Apparently being filthy rich meant you couldn't enjoy color.

When he reached the upstairs landing he made his way toward the west wing where Evie's bedroom was located. His senses were on high alert, listening for sounds from behind her closed door. But there was nothing. It was rare for Evie to sit in silence. She thrived in noise and chaos, usually choosing to do her work with something blasting in her ears.

He also figured she'd have had plenty of time to work up a head of steam after their kiss in the kitchen. Evie wasn't quiet when she was angry or upset. She paced, or tossed things around, or muttered under her breath.

He knocked on her door and waited for a response.

There was nothing.

"Evie?" he asked. "Open up. We need to talk."

But still there was no response.

His heart thudded in his chest as he put his weapon down at his side and tried the knob. It was locked.

"Evie, I'm giving you fair warning. If you don't open the door I'm breaking the door down."

He tried not to let fear get him. He knew the French doors were a vulnerable entry point. He never should have let her come back upstairs alone. What if Taber already had her?

Without a second thought his foot made contact with the door, and it splintered open.

"Evie!" he called out again as he made the

perimeter, checking the closets and bathroom along the way. There was no sign of her. No note. Nothing. She was just—gone.

The French doors were unlocked from the inside and he swore.

Cal knew the house, inside and out. He'd spent countless hours there, visiting the family, vacationing at the beach, and playing golf at the course down the road. He'd familiarized himself even more by studying the security system and the plans in place for an emergency evacuation.

If Taber didn't have her it meant she'd left of her own volition. And if that was the case he was going to wring her neck for putting her life in danger. He hadn't been kidding when he'd told her they were going to stick together like glue. Where she went, he would be. And vice versa. That included their sleeping arrangements. She wasn't going to be happy about it—he wasn't that happy about it either because she was a temptation that would be hard to resist—but the only question she should have was what side of the bed she should sleep on. That's how close they needed to be at all times.

But it was a necessity. Her bedroom was a security nightmare. It was on the second floor, and a veranda ran the entire length of that wing of the house. Double staircases ran all the way to the third floor, and her bedroom had a wall of windows and a French door along the entire side of one wall. Huge palm trees surrounded the house, which provided cover for anyone who shouldn't be there, and there was a two-hundred-year-old live oak with strong and extended branches centered in the back courtyard.

He knew from experience how easy it was to jump onto a branch from the balcony and shimmy down to the ground. It was also easy to climb when trying to sneak into the house. The scenery was beautiful—a clear view of the ocean on a sunny day. But it was paradise to anyone who wanted to get in. And for someone like Taber, it was like wrapping Evangeline up like a present and handing her over.

The bedroom across the hall and at the opposite end of the wing was a much better and safer choice. He could set up security precautions to give them time to escape if someone breached the house.

He took a deep breath and calmed his mind, doing another pass through the bedroom. It was a room that suited the real Evangeline. Not stuffy and closed off like she pretended to be. But vibrant and full of life and color. It made him think of something a sultan and his harem might enjoy.

The bed was a massive four-poster monstrosity, dominating the room, and the comforter a rich blue silk. Sheers in different shades of blue and turquoise were draped from one corner to the other and pillows were piled high on the bed. Rugs with the same shades of turquoise were scattered along the hardwood floors, and there was a sitting area with a delicate settee in pure white and a chair upholstered in blue with thin gold stripes. Soft white sheers hung in place of curtains, but they were no protection against anyone who wanted to see in. It was the only room in the house with color.

There were no signs of struggle. She was a neat and organized creature of habit. She hadn't always been that way. It's as if a switch had been flipped that day ten years before.

The room was full of books—all kinds of books—from romance novels to technology guides, to memoirs. The shelves and every available surface were overflowing with books. And a lone, battered laptop sat closed on her desk. The pang of regret was sharp.

He checked his phone. There was no contact from any of the agents he had watching the house. She'd slipped out. Unnoticed. Unprotected. How did she do it?

He did another pass through the bathroom and noticed the clothes she'd been wearing down in the kitchen. They were folded neatly on the side of the tub. He went back over to the French doors and opened them, stepping out onto the balcony.

He dialed a number on his phone and waited for the answer.

"James," the agent said.

"Evangeline is gone," Cal said. "Give me a report. Who's got eyes on the back of the house?"

"Curtis," James said. "But we had a slight hiccup. He's in one of the boats watching from the water, but the tide shifted and the winds picked up. He got set off course and lost visual for a few minutes."

"A storm is going to be coming in tonight," Cal said. "If you've got boats out there you better make sure the agents in them are experienced sailors. Things are going to get rough, and that's exactly the time that Taber will strike."

"Yes, sir," James said.

"She went off her balcony and climbed down the tree. I can see her footprints on the sand. Do you see her?"

"I don't have a visual," James said. "She must be hidden behind the rocks. There's a cove that's pretty secluded."

"I feel like I'm keeping a pretty good hold of my temper by not coming down there and beating the hell out of all of you, and then finding people competent enough to keep track of one woman."

"It won't happen again, sir," James said.

Cal disconnected. His anger was directed at Atticus. This is what happened when he pulled in local field agents instead of hand-selected agents. Dynamis agents would never have made such a mistake.

The smell of the sea was strong, and he could feel the heaviness of the rain in the air. He looked over the white railing of the balcony and saw the footprints in the sand below. He swore, thinking that holding on to Evangeline was like holding a fistful of sand. He could practically feel it slipping out of his grasp.

He closed and locked the French doors behind him and kept his weapon in his hand as he jogged back down the stairs toward the back of the house.

He followed the footsteps down the beach, relieved to see there was only one set. The closest neighbor was almost a mile in either direction—

the Lockwoods had complete privacy in their little stretch of paradise. No trash littered the ground and the sand was white and pristine.

His walk had turned into a run by the time he came upon the outcropping of rocks. The footprints disappeared right at the smallest boulder, signifying she'd started climbing at that point. And then he heard the squeal and splash and his heartbeat went into overdrive. His first thought was that she'd fallen and hit her head on the rocks. His second thought was that someone had been hiding on the other side and attacked her.

He climbed the rocks, staying to the outer edge, thinking he'd have the advantage by attacking the culprit from above. He held his weapon up and waited patiently, moving slowly toward the sounds that were getting louder.

There was a split in the rocks—large enough for a man to fit through—so he hunkered down for a better view and to assess the situation. What he saw was nothing his imagination could've conjured in his wildest dreams. It was a spectacular hiding place. Or a hell of a place to be ambushed.

A small lagoon was nestled inside the rock formation, completely invisible to the outside world unless you were perched above like he was.

A natural waterfall rushed down the rocks and into a crystal-clear pool. It couldn't have been deep, maybe a few feet, because he could see all the way to the bottom.

And there was Evangeline, climbing the rocks until she was at the top of the waterfall, her hair slicked back from her face and her body barely covered in a skimpy bathing suit. The baggy clothes she'd spent the last decade in were an injustice to her. She was lush and beautiful, and there was sheer joy on her face as she jumped into the lagoon below, laughing as she came up from the depths of the water.

His heart was racing a mile a minute and he laid his head against the cool rocks to find his balance. She'd scared years off his life. Maybe that reckless girl hadn't disappeared after all.

He holstered his weapon in the small of his back and stepped through the opening of the rocks. She didn't notice him, at least not right away. Not until his shadow crossed her face.

She gasped and looked up at him, her hand shielding her eyes so she could see who'd intruded on her space.

"Have you lost your mind?" he asked as calmly as he could manage. "Do you not understand there's a madman after you? A man who tortured and dismembered the last witness who tried to testify against him?"

He saw the fright on her face before she masked it with a look of indifference.

"You said the house is surrounded by agents and we're protected. And this is a completely secluded spot. I felt perfectly safe."

"I also told you that we were to stick together like glue," he said through gritted teeth. "I can't protect you if I'm not with you. He could have had you in his scope from a mile off."

"Ridiculous," she said, treading water. "That doesn't fit his profile. If he wants to capture and torture me that means he's an up-close-and-personal kind of killer. He won't take a cheap shot."

"Which is exactly why you don't need to be more than an arm's length away," he said, stripping off his shirt. He unbuckled his belt next and found a perverse pleasure in the worry on her face.

"What are you doing?" she asked, treading backward toward the waterfall. She bit her lip nervously.

He pushed down his jeans until he was in his boxers and laid his weapon on one of the lower rocks so he could reach it easily. "I'm getting in the water. What does it look like I'm doing? Sometimes I feel like words come out of my mouth but you're not actually listening."

"I've heard enough words coming out of your mouth to last a lifetime," she said, sarcastically. "I try not to listen more than I have to."

"Then I'll repeat myself again. Where you go, I go. If you're going to swim, I'm going to swim. If you're on the couch, I'm on the couch. If you're in the shower, I'm close enough to hand you the soap."

She gasped and her eyes narrowed. "My father could not have approved of this."

"It was his idea," Cal said. "And I don't report to your father. Atticus Cameron is scarier than your father could ever hope to be."

"And how am I supposed to sleep?"

He grinned, but there was no humor in it. "I get to be the big spoon. Does that answer your question?"

She disappeared under the water and he could see the ribbons of her hair as she went under the waterfall. It was fine with him. She could come to grips with reality however she needed to. It didn't change the fact that this was her reality now.

He took the opportunity to swim a couple of laps across the lagoon and back, keeping an eye on the rocks and the weather. He hated that his presence had taken the joy from her face that had been there just a few minutes before. But it couldn't be helped. There was too much between them. Too much history, too much anger, and too much attraction.

When she surfaced again her eyes met his, clear and dry, and his breath caught at the sheer beauty of her. No makeup. No persona. Just Evangeline.

"We don't want to stay out too long," he said. "The weather is going to turn bad before too long."

"How do you know?" she asked, looking at the sky. "It looks clear and sunny to me."

"Because the wind shifted and the waves changed," he said. "I grew up on the water. My dad was a shrimper in the South Carolina Lowcountry. I could pilot a boat long before I got a driver's license, and I could read the signs of upcoming weather before I started school."

"So how come you're a hacker instead of a shrimper?" she asked, curiosity written across her face.

It was the first time she'd ever asked about his childhood. When they'd been kids she'd just accepted him for who he was. She'd never commented on his drawl or that his manners weren't refined and his clothes didn't have designer labels. And he'd never bothered to offer up the information. As far as he was concerned that part of his life was over, and if he tried hard enough, he could pretend it never happened at all.

Cal shrugged and swam closer to the waterfall and to her, close enough he could feel the splashes on his face.

"My dad liked to drink," he said. "He had big fists, and he liked dangerous waters and rough bars. He was killed in a knife fight when I was seven. He was drunk and picked a fight with the wrong man. My mother was relieved I think. I guess I was too."

Her mouth opened in an *O* of surprise, but she stayed silent, watching him out of those eyes that had always been too big and too wise for her face.

"We'd been poor when my dad was alive," he said, remembering back to the two-room cabin they'd lived in along the marsh. "After he died we were really poor. Mom went out to find work. Sometimes she came home, and sometimes she didn't. That left me to my own devices. I'd always done well in school, even skipped the first grade, and the first time they put a computer in my hands I thought I'd died and gone to heaven. When I wasn't in school I was at the library using the ones there. It was then I realized that I could do everything I needed to do to make life easier with just the stroke of a few keys. I made it my mission to get my own setup."

He wasn't sure why he was telling her all this. He'd just opened his mouth and the words started pouring out. It had been a long time since he'd thought of those early days—the days before Robert Lockwood had tracked him down and taken him into custody.

His smile was grim. "That's when I started to take a turn toward the dark side. I was a ten-year-old kid with no supervision. I was big for my age, and I knew how to fight to get what I wanted. I also knew how to steal and keep out of sight from the law. I made friends with grifters and thieves. I hacked into my first bank before my eleventh birthday. I was never a stupid kid. I kept going to school. I knew that if I stopped I'd be wanted for truancy. I had no idea where my mother was at that point, so I made one up.

"I set up different accounts, siphoning money from different places so it would take longer to track down. And then I hired this woman, Mary

Louise Cobb, to pretend she was my mother. They wouldn't exactly let a ten-year-old rent an apartment by himself, so she and I made a deal. She got a nice kickback and she left me to my own devices and never asked questions. It was a setup that worked well until your father broke down my door."

"Wow," she said. "I can't imagine having that kind of ingenuity at ten."

"Survival skills kick in when you need them," he said.

"Whatever happened to your mother?"

"I have no idea," he said. "She never came looking for me. I was just a mouth to feed, and she was having a hard enough time filling her own. It worked out for the best, at least until I was fourteen. Your dad gave me a chance to walk the straight and narrow or go to prison. It seemed like the best option at the time."

She looked at him strangely, and he wondered what she was thinking. But she didn't ask any more questions. Instead she said, "We should probably go back to the house."

Chapter Eight

Cal was driving her crazy. And he was doing it on purpose. Jerk.

Something had shifted between them. They'd been in a battle for years, equally matched in the hardheadedness department, and it was as if they'd both come to an unspoken resolve. She'd spent years trying to replace her love of him with anger, but she was tired. It was hard work to keep that level of hatred in your heart. Especially since she'd loved him for as long as she could remember.

Seeing him again, wanting him again, loving him again…she just didn't have the strength to go through it all. He'd rejected her. That's what it really came down to. It hadn't been a rejection of her looks or her affections, he'd rejected her at the core of who she was.

She'd spent years fantasizing about his reaction when he found out what she was capable of. That she was his equal in every way. She thought it would open his eyes and make him really see her. That she was no longer the little girl who followed him around like a puppy. But a woman who could match him in every way. She'd been sorely disappointed that the reality hadn't lived up to the fantasy. But it was her own fault. She recognized now the girl who'd been starved for attention from the men in her life. To be able to prove that she was just as capable and just as worthy of the love, time and attention that her father gave to his agents. She'd gone about it the wrong way, and there was nothing she could do to change the past.

She was done being held under Cal's thumb. If she had to confess her sins to her father she would. But being around Cal again had opened something up inside of her. Even his kiss had been like a veil being removed from her eyes. And she was done living half a life. She was done not being who she was meant to be.

Cal had set up shop in the kitchen. His computers were lined up like soldiers on the big breakfast table and he sat at the keyboard like a king, his fingers moving from one to the other as naturally as some people might breathe.

She knew what it felt like. Knew the rush of power that one tiny command could bring. And there he sat, looking better than he had any right to and just as dangerous. His hair was tousled and a little long around the collar and ears. After they'd come back from the beach he'd changed into a pair of loose-fitting lounge pants and a white T-shirt that hugged his biceps and chest like a second skin. His forearms were strong, the muscles there prominent, and she wanted to get a closer look at the tattoos that ran from shoulder to wrist.

Cal was built like a boxer, with well-defined muscles and an athletic build that made women take a second look whenever he walked into a room.

She was losing her mind. She felt like a teenage girl with a serious case of infatuation, and all she could think about was kissing him again. She went to the fridge to grab a cold bottle of water, looking for a distraction.

She'd always considered herself abnormal, an anomaly in the relationship department. It was always supposed to be Cal for her. She knew it as well as she knew to breathe. No one else had ever captured her attention like he had. She'd never gone through the teenage girl stage where she'd felt the flutter of butterflies any time a boy looked in her direction. There was a soul connection between them, even if he didn't realize it because he couldn't see her as anything more than the child she'd been.

After he'd broken her heart she'd thrown herself into schoolwork, going through two master's programs as if they'd been elementary school. It hadn't been enough to keep her busy so she'd decided to go on and get her PhD, thinking Cal would come back around once he saw she'd grown up. That he would give her the chance to redeem all the wrongs that had been done.

But it hadn't happened. Her father had let it slip about Cal's marriage, almost as an afterthought. He'd been frustrated because Cal put in for vacation leave last minute so he could take a couple of weeks for a honeymoon, and it had left him shorthanded.

The news had been devastating to Evangeline. She remembered that day in her father's office in Technicolor. Time had slowed down—the way he'd been standing behind his desk, shuffling through papers and muttering under his breath in aggravation. The way the grandfather clock had chimed, as if it knew how important it was to etch such a moment in her memory forever.

He'd met her on a job—an accident of fate—as she'd occupied the apartment next to a target the team was keeping tabs on. Julie had been completely opposite of Cal. She'd been a kindergarten teacher and visited her parents every weekend. She'd been a nice girl who'd fallen in love with the man who'd saved her life, and she'd thrown caution to the wind and eloped with him a week later.

Hearing her father utter those words had been the second worst day of her life. She didn't even think her father had noticed when she'd turned around and walked out of his office. That she'd left the house to go back to campus without a goodbye.

All she wanted was for the pain to go away, so she'd gone to a bar a block from campus and gotten ridiculously drunk. She'd also run into one of her graduate professors and used her skills of deception to make her think she was experienced when it came to men. She hadn't been. She'd just been looking for someone, anyone else to fill the void.

And she'd gotten exactly what she'd been

looking for. There'd been something about that professor that reminded her of Cal. Maybe his build or the way he'd walked or quirked his head to the side when he was thinking. But there was enough that she could pretend. She'd used him shamelessly for a few weeks. And then she'd walked away with shame and guilt. She'd stopped pursuing doctoral work and found a job that she was way too qualified for, settling down into the life she felt she deserved.

Since then her life had been quiet. There had been no other men. She went to work and came home. And when the sun went down she opened her computer, making sure the walls she'd built to keep Cal out of her life were in place. She knew he kept tabs on her. Was keeping watch on every digital move she made. And it brought her a thrill to know she was good enough to deceive him.

Besides, the tables had turned. She was only doing a little side work from time to time, assisting certain nonprofit organizations in their fundraising so they could help more people. The way she looked at it, she was helping everyone involved. The mega rich she siphoned funds from needed the tax deductions and didn't even realize what charitable contributions they were making. And the charitable organizations publically thanked their largest donors, and it wasn't like the wealthy were going to take it back if they didn't remember making a sizable contribution.

She looked at it as a kind of penance. A way to give back and atone for all the wrongs she'd done before. And it gave her a thrill at the same time to know she'd bested Cal. He'd moved on, living his own life. She could do the same.

She'd decided after Cal's marriage and her own disastrous attempt at love that it was better to feel nothing than to feel too much. And maybe she was one of those people who weren't meant to love or be loved. Relationships required trust. She wasn't sure she had the capability to trust anyone. She had no desire to get caught up in a game of mistrust and untruths, and the best way to avoid that problem was to not put herself in the situation.

Cal's betrayal—or what she'd seen as his betrayal—had devastated her. He'd thought he'd been doing the right thing. And he had been, the best way he knew how. He'd treated her like a child when she'd wanted him to see her as a woman. As his equal. His mate.

Now, ten years later, those same urges that had formed when she was young were back in full force. She didn't like the fact that her heart didn't seem to care that she didn't trust him. The heart and the mind didn't always agree, and this time the urges of her heart were stronger than her mind.

"You got some sun today," he said, looking at her over his screen. "You should know better by now. You've never been able to tan."

"But I keep on trying," she said, taking a sip of water.

"We've got to talk about earlier," he said, his expression serious.

She froze. She didn't want to talk about the kiss. She hadn't been able to think about anything else, but that didn't mean she wanted to discuss it in minute detail. Or worse, hear about how much he regretted it and that it would never happen again.

"What about earlier?" she asked, a little defensively.

"I know you're irritated at this whole situation," he said. "And I can't say I blame you. I wouldn't take kindly to people barging into my life and keeping me on what is essentially house arrest for an unforeseeable amount of time."

"Oh," she said, taken off guard by a different conversation than what she'd been expecting. She let out a slow breath of relief. "Yeah, well…

it doesn't seem like there's much I can do about it."

"You can't do that again," he said. "Don't try to slip past me or any of the agents assigned to protect you. If you want to go to the beach we'll go if there's an all clear. But the best thing we can do is stay inside and wait Taber out. Actually, the best thing we could do is for me to take you to a safe house and not tell anyone where we've gone."

She looked at him closely, trying to figure out why his tone of voice had changed. It was obvious Cal had gotten specific orders to keep her here, and he didn't like it. And then it clicked.

"But if we did that I couldn't draw Taber out into the open," she said, watching the myriad of emotions cross Cal's face.

"Atticus is keeping a bead on Taber," Cal said. "Taber took out a target in Dallas that I've just confirmed was connected to Senator Biddle. Amir was the head of AeroNaut. A big-time government contractor. Senator Biddle was head of the Senate Defense Committee. Atticus says we might have a few days at most before Taber finds time for you in his busy killing schedule."

"So it was Atticus that wanted to use me as bait?" she asked, arching a brow.

Cal hesitated and she knew the truth. She

knew her father better than anyone. He loved her, she knew in her soul that he did. But his mission in life had been greater than a wife and daughter. Saving the world wasn't conducive to deep and meaningful relationships. His want for her to be safe versus letting a monster roam free would have been an internal struggle he couldn't have compromised on.

"I see," she said, smiling wryly.

"Evie, your father—"

"You don't have to explain my father to me," she said, interrupting. "I know him better than anyone and I would've expected no less."

"You're the only one," Cal said under his breath, but loud enough that she could hear him. "Besides, Atticus told him no."

She laughed at that. "Oh, I would've liked to have seen that. Not many people in this world have the guts to tell Robert Lockwood no."

"We'll stay here for a few more days and try to get a bead on Taber. If he slips off the radar then you and I are out of here. We should be getting a couple of extra agents in too."

"I guess it's good we're camped out in this mausoleum instead of my place. There's room for everyone."

"Do you want to come see what I'm doing?" he asked, fingers flying across the keyboard.

"I believe me standing over there violates my probation."

"Evie," he said, rubbing the back of my neck. "I'm a pretty good judge of character. Now you and I both know that I've been watching your online activity over the last decade. And you and I both also know that despite the program I've designed and implemented, someone with your talents could have found a fail-safe and waltzed right through it."

She couldn't help the smirk. It had taken her almost two years to meticulously work through his system without tripping herself up and getting caught. But she'd done it.

"Now what I don't know is what you've been doing with your remarkable talents. So nice job on that front, though I admit I could have found out if I'd wanted. But whatever your sideline hobby is, it must have a more noble outcome than your previous work because I haven't been able to trace you in the underground."

She couldn't help but taunt him a little. "Maybe I just outsmarted you."

"I don't think so," he said, answering her grin. "I've learned in my line of work that sometimes it's best to let sleeping dogs lie. I could have countered your workarounds and dug into your life. More than I already have. But I didn't."

"Bully for you," she said, shrugging and walking toward his monitors. "I can't imagine the lack of depth in your life if you could spend ten years digging into my boring day-to-day routine. I think that says more about you than it does about me. Now show me what you're doing before you explode."

He was silent for a few seconds, but it felt like an eternity. "I had plenty to keep me busy during the last decade. More than I thought I could handle most of the time."

She swallowed painfully, hating to hear the regret in his voice. "I'm sorry about your wife. Dad told me what happened."

"I'm told it's a chance we all take," he said. "Look what happened to Atticus's wife and daughter. Lesson learned." He turned the monitor so she could see and she figured he was done talking about his wife. "The Pentagon has changed some of their security since the last time I got into their system."

She wanted to tell him she knew, but pressed her lips together tighter.

"Senator Biddle and the Defense Committee

were taking bids from government contractors for a new missile. It would appear on the surface to be business as usual. Contractors would send their bids to the committee, and then the committee would award the job to whoever could implement the technology and meet the deadline.

"But it didn't take long to realize that the initial proposal to the committee wasn't what would really be delivered. We're talking stealth drones with the capacity to carry a nuclear weapon with enough power to wipe out an area the size of France, Germany, and Spain put together. The contract is worth billions."

"And that's more than enough to kill for," she said. She fought the urge to move closer and read over his shoulder.

"From what I've found John Amir at Aero-Naut was the favorite to receive the contract. He and Senator Biddle are friends and allies. They've done several deals in the past."

"Except now they're both dead."

"Right you are," he said.

"So who are the other players?" she asked.

"AeroNaut has the clout, experience, and the design, but Amir was the face and genius of that company. They could move forward without him, but I wouldn't want to do the deal with something that sensitive on the line and no leadership.

"Boulder would be up next," he said. "They're based out of Atlanta. Biddle had a few notes on their submitted designs, but if he has any classified documents they're not digital and I don't have access. Biddle was set to meet with Boulder's acting CEO, Jenson Walker, the day after his murder to go over the contracts. They're in the transition process so they don't have the same stability as a company like AeroNaut.

"Boulder's strength is in its aircraft designs, not necessarily in missiles, but they've secretly brought on some of the best engineers in the nation to help them land the contract. They're keeping everything close to the vest, and I'm still working through their security. It's top notch. Should take me another day before I can get in and see their designs."

She grunted, absorbed in reading the symbols scrolling rapidly across the screen. He'd used a data encryption program that was slowly working its way through Boulder's system like an invisible worm redirecting and rewriting code as it went as a subterfuge. She itched to get her fingers on the keyboard and take it apart to see how he'd created it.

"Am I boring you?" he asked.

"Oh, no," she said. "Just enjoying the beauty of your artwork."

"I think that's the first time you've ever complimented me."

"Don't let it go to your head," she said. "Who's next?"

"DyniCorp."

"Interesting," she said.

"In what way?"

"My father invited me to dinner with a couple of contractors from DyniCorp," she said. "I assumed they were on his most-wanted-bachelor list so I politely declined the invitation."

Cal coughed, but she saw his smile. "They've been a powerhouse in the industry the last five years," he said. "The company was built slowly, taking on smaller projects that could be done well instead of biting off more than they could chew. Their reputation is solid."

"That doesn't mean they don't need the money. There's not a lot of people who wouldn't risk their reputation for a billion-dollar contract. There's a lot of chaos that ensues when someone as important as a senator gets murdered. Depending on what side of the aisle you're sitting on, the blame game will target whoever the opposite side is trying to vilify. The chances of the true responsible party taking the fall for this is slim. It bothers me there's a connection with my father. Maybe that's how they've been keeping tabs."

"It's a good hunch to follow," he said. "I'm in the process of building a secondary program to infiltrate their financials. Whoever they've got on cybersecurity is top notch. I haven't been able to uncover who that is as of yet."

"Which bothers you," she said. "There's something else that bothers you too. I can tell."

"I don't like not knowing who I'm up against," he said. "That's the first issue. The second is that Dynamis Security holds a large percentage of shares in DyniCorp. Atticus is going to be pissed if they're the culprit. That means they'll have played all of us like a masterful game of chess. And I don't particularly like being anyone's pawn."

Something struck her and she hesitated, wondering if she should voice her thoughts aloud.

"What is it?" he asked.

"I think we'd be naïve not to consider that Atticus could be as involved in this as anyone. He's got the perfect setup and the perfect cover. He could have easily hired Taber and left the crumb trail to each of the victims. These targets are important men with high-level security. They're not easy to kill. But two of them are dead. And what better way for Taber to reach me than for Atticus to have us right where he wants us both."

"I don't know whether I should be impressed or pissed," he said.

"Let's go with impressed," she said. "I've seen far too little of that from you in my lifetime." Her smile was thin and impertinent.

He snorted out a laugh and leaned back in the chair so it stood on two legs. "You're thinking like an agent. That's good. Those instincts will keep you safe. But you don't know Atticus like I do. There are a few people I trust in this world, who I'd lay everything down for and do a job without question. He's one of those people. Atticus is the most solid guy I know. He doesn't flinch, and he doesn't compromise his principles. Not ever."

"Is my father one of those few?" she asked.

Cal opened his mouth to speak, but hesitated. At one point in his life he would have said yes. But Robert played the government's game. And that didn't always mean that it was the *right* game.

Evangeline blew out a breath. "Well that's good to know."

"It would depend on the circumstance," he

said. "But he's your father. I don't believe he'd ever intentionally put you in harm's way without a fail-safe."

"So you're my fail-safe?" she asked.

"Among other things," he said. "I'd never put your life at risk, Evie. You've got to trust me on that one. Keeping you alive is the most important job I have, even more than finding out who's behind this. If it came to the point where I had to choose your safety or bring down a company that could potentially ruin my career and what Atticus Cameron has built, guess which I'd choose?"

She went perfectly still, her hands clenching into fists at her sides. She wanted to believe him. Wanted to think that she was that important to him—that he'd risk everything for her safety. Promises of that magnitude were easily broken when push came to shove. Her father had always told her to look out for herself first, because no one else ever would. She had to assume he'd given the same advice to Cal.

"I'm still gathering information at this point," he said. "I'm breaking down the walls at Langley. That won't take as long as breaching the security at Boulder and DyniCorp."

"Sad isn't it?" she asked.

"It doesn't pay to work for the government," Cal said. "I should know. They were lucky to have me, though I didn't exactly have a choice at the time. It's all gone to hell since I left."

"You could still be out on your own," she said. "There's a lot of money on the private side of things."

"Atticus pays me a fortune," he said. "No one is hacking into the systems at Dynamis. Besides, I never have to wear a suit or sit in front of congressional committees. It's in my contract. As far as I'm concerned it's my dream job. And I never would have been a government stooge if I hadn't been indebted to your father. I didn't actually think he was going to let me retire. A lifetime of indentured servitude with mediocre equipment and no vision."

"Something is better than nothing," she said. "I should know."

"Life is what you make it, Evie. The last ten years are what you created. There was still life going on around you even though you chose a different path. You got your kicks in the dark, sipping from an eyedropper when you could have found your courage and fortitude and used your gifts. But you chose to pout for the last ten years and go stale. That's on you. Not on me. But if it makes you feel better to blame me then have at it."

She blew out a breath. What was the point in bringing up the past? "It was a long time ago," she said. "Let's just forget it."

"Fine," Cal said. "We know that Senator Biddle met with Deputy Director Frank Reed the morning of his death in Reed's office. All of those meetings are monitored and recorded. I'm trying to get access to the video."

Cal rubbed his eyes and then ran a hand through his hair. "I could use the help, Evie. This would go a lot faster if we were each working on it."

The laugh that escaped her throat was brittle with emotion. "You know, Cal, through all the years we've known each other, I never realized you have that kind of cruelty in you. So what? I sit down at the computer to help and then all of a sudden you decide to turn me in for what happened a decade ago. I don't trust you."

"Says the woman who was kissing me only a few hours ago."

"Trusting and making out are two very different things. You don't have to have one to get the other. And there's nothing wrong with me kissing you. I enjoyed it. And I assume you did too. We're both adults. And we might as well do something if we're going to be stuck with each other."

He looked at her like she'd grown a second head. "That may be one of the saddest things I've ever heard. You're not really that hard, Evie. Why are you trying to pretend you are?"

"My feelings are my own. I don't owe you anything else. But my future—what there is or isn't of it—is in your hands. So you can see why I'd pass on your very tempting offer to entrap myself."

"You really think I'd do that to you?" She was surprised by the current of anger in his voice and the hardness that came into his eyes.

"I don't know you well enough to know what you would do. But I wouldn't trust you to do any differently. Better to be safe than sorry."

He stood up abruptly, the chair skidding back across the floor, and he came toward her slowly, stalking her like a cat would its prey. He stopped several feet in front of her and she wanted to flinch at the hurt and anger in his face. But that's what he wanted her to see. Cal had spent too long in covert ops. He was a consummate actor.

"Are you afraid of me?" he asked.

She wasn't. Had never been afraid of him. And that put her at ease. She hadn't realized how stiff she was.

"I'm not afraid of you. I've been taking care of myself a long time. But I don't know what your game is either. You've never been one to show your hand."

"What good would that do?" he asked. "You might as well wave a white flag in defeat."

"True. And yet here we stand. Knowing an opponent's strengths and weaknesses is essential."

He nodded. "Know thy enemy. Is that what we are, Evangeline? Opponents?"

She didn't realize how different her full name sounded coming from his lips. He'd always called her Evie.

"Being opponents would mean that I care one way or the other," she said, shrugging. "You're just a guy here to protect me on my father's orders. Nothing more. Nothing less."

He moved in close, but she didn't back down. Wouldn't back down. "You can keep lying to yourself, Evie. But you can't lie to me. Your body can't lie to me."

And then he kissed her. It wasn't the same as the kiss they'd shared earlier that morning. This was a kiss that scorched her very soul. She could taste his anger, yes, but there was more beneath the surface. Desire—need—frustration. And a longing so desperate it almost brought her to her knees.

What was happening? When had this happened? She'd loved him since she was a young girl, despite trying to hate him. Was it possible that there could be more between them?

Her fingers pressed hard into the muscles of his arms, and she moaned as his arms came around her and pulled her even closer. The room was spinning and she wasn't sure if she was even drawing a breath any longer. There was just Cal. Everything else ceased to exist.

He pulled away and she fell into him, feeling the void of his touch immediately. His gaze never left hers, his pupils so large she could only see a thin ring of brown at the edges. There was something electric between them. And so many things that had never been spoken. She was wondering how they could ever redeem all that had been lost between them when he threw her a lifeline.

"I've got to get back to work," he said, his voice hoarse. "You're welcome to pull up a stool and help. Either way, stay in the room and away from the windows."

She nodded and he released her, stepping

away. She already felt the loss. Then she drew in a deep breath and moved toward the monitor, her blood singing for reasons more than just the kiss.

Chapter Nine

The storm broke sometime during the night. Rain and wind and thunder.

But Evangeline slept peacefully beside him. In her sleep, at least, she trusted him. He hadn't been kidding when he'd told her they wouldn't be separated until Taber was caught. She'd only looked slightly panicked as they'd stood on opposite sides of the bed, staring down at the silk-covered space between them. He'd always admired her courage.

As for him, sleeping beside Evangeline was purgatory. He deserved the punishment. He was sure of it. He'd given up on any semblance of sleep and lay still on his back, staring up at the ceiling and watching the play of shadows as lightning lit the night sky. His sweats and T-shirt scratched against his skin, and even though the windows were closed he could feel the humidity from the storm outside.

They were in the room he usually stayed in whenever he came to visit Robert, at the opposite end of the wing from Evie's bedroom. He didn't stay there often, but when Nadine had been alive she'd always made sure he felt at home.

The bedroom sat at the corner of the house and had two banks of windows—one that faced the gardens in the side yard and another that faced the ocean. There was no balcony, but the windows opened and it was an easy hop onto the roof if an escape needed to be made. He'd already made sure he'd left the window unlocked and ropes anchored to the roof if they needed a quick getaway.

The fan whirred lazily overhead, the noise seemingly loud between the rumbles of thunder. His senses were primed. Palm trees scraped against the windows and the wind howled with fury.

There'd been no updates from Atticus or any of the agents on lookout. Not that he'd expected there to be. Taber had to get from Dallas to Florida. That was going to take a little time, depending on what mode of transportation he used. But he could be there as early as sometime that day or as late as tomorrow or the next day if there were no more stops to make along the way.

A crack of thunder followed by a flash of lightning so bright he thought it hit the house sounded, and a loud crash and glass breaking came from somewhere close by.

He rolled out of bed, grabbing the weapon he'd had under his pillow, and he shook Evangeline awake, keeping a hand over her mouth so she wouldn't make any noise. The whites of her eyes were bright as she stared at him in sleepy confusion.

"Ssh," he said, putting a finger to his lips.

She nodded and he let her go, and he gestured for her to get low on the ground and keep cover. She shook her head and opened the drawer of the bedside table, pulling out a Glock in matte black. He raised his eyebrows because he hadn't seen her put it there, but he knew she could shoot as well as any agent. One of the perks of being Robert Lockwood's daughter.

He could stand there and argue with her to stay put, but it'd just be wasting time. So he narrowed his eyes and moved in close so she could hear him.

"Stay close and stay behind me," he said. He

waited until she nodded in agreement and then headed to the bedroom door.

The knob was cool beneath his touch and he opened the door slowly so he could peek into the hallway. The wind howled and there was an incessant banging somewhere down the hall.

He moved with precision, his bare feet silent against the cool marble floor of the hallway. Evie shadowed close behind him, her steps as silent as his. Robert had made sure she received as much training growing up as his agents, maybe more so, and he trusted her to have his back. They moved to the room next door and he opened it, clearing the area quickly, and then he closed the door behind him.

They repeated the motions twice more as they made their way down the long hallway. And then they finally stood in front of Evangeline's door. The wind and banging were louder now, but he'd had to make sure the other rooms were clear first before bursting into Evie's room looking for battle. People died because of their impatience.

There was resistance as he tried to open the door—the wind pushing against it—but he cleared the entryway and stayed to the perimeter of the room as he searched for any threats. But it was pretty clear what had happened. The rug and bed were soaked through with rain and a large tree limb had broken through the French doors. One of the doors banged against an armoire, and shards of glass rattled in the frame.

"Well this is a mess," she whispered, lowering her weapon.

He moved to the balcony and crept around the edges, but it was impossible to see but a few inches in front of his face with the heavy rain.

He moved to the bathroom for a last look, checked the closets, and under the bed, but there was no one there but the two of them.

"I guess it's a good thing you weren't sleeping here tonight," he said, looking at the sharp glass on the bed.

"I'm trying not to think about that part," she said, her eyes transfixed.

"We're going to need plastic bags and duct tape," he said. "We'll clean up what we can and then seal this room off. It's an even more vulnerable entry point now."

"The housekeepers have a supply closet at the end of the hall," she said, looking down at her bare feet. "We should probably put on shoes."

"Yeah," he said. "Let me call this in. You put on some shoes. I saw some sneakers in the closet over there."

"What about you?" she asked.

"Come on," he said. "I don't want to leave you here alone. We'll grab the supplies on the way back."

He made the call into headquarters and gave a status update while he slipped his feet into his own shoes. The bad news was the weather had sent all the agents on watercraft to shore for safety. Lockwood's closest neighbor was out of the country, and the agents had set up a command post in the guesthouse. The problem was they were relying solely on the interior cameras and sound since their visibility was nonexistent around the perimeter of the house.

They found oversized trash bags and duct tape and headed back to the room. It was wet, messy work, and they were both soaked to the skin in minutes as they pushed the tree limb back outside.

"We need to soak up some of this water before we put up the plastic," she said. "Nothing will stick."

"We need to get the glass out of the way first. Then we can dry things off without cutting ourselves to pieces." He held up his arm so she could see the shallow gash that had sliced him while they'd been moving the limb.

"You have control issues," she said, putting her hands on her hips.

He squared off with her. "If I have control issues then you have common sense issues. Good Lord, Evie, stop trying to fight me on every issue and start working with me."

They worked in silence for several minutes, picking up the largest pieces of glass and knocking out some that was hanging dangerously from the French doors. Evie came in with towels to soak up the water from the walls and floor, and then they spread the trash bags taut across the open space and secured them until it was completely covered.

"Say I start working with you for real," she said once they were finished. "Different than this afternoon. More. Then what happens? Do I wait and wonder whether or not you're going to use what you know against me? Say I do something you don't like on a job and then you've got the power to blackmail me with my past. That doesn't seem like a fun way to live."

"Nope," he said, his heart pounding in his chest with a combination of frustration and anger. She was driving him crazy. "You'd have to learn to trust me. Plain and simple. Just like I'd have to trust you not to ever go back to the old ways. To be a team player instead of looking out only for yourself. You do the jobs we do and everyone relies on each other. None of us have time to question whether or not we might get stabbed in the back by a team member. So it seems like a pretty even trade from where I stand."

"Except your trust, or lack thereof, won't send *you* to prison for the rest of your life," she said. "I don't have that luxury."

"You know as well as I do that you've eliminated all traces of the Black Lily. As far as the governments of the world are concerned, she never existed. Sounds familiar to me. My past disappeared too. If we'd both stayed on the crooked path maybe we could have shared a prison cell."

She smiled for the first time. "Just two legends whispered about in the underground. A legacy that will eventually die out altogether. Sounds like a fresh start to me. A way to knock off the rust."

"The work I saw you do today didn't look rusty at all," he said, arching a brow. "It looked like you'd never left the game."

"It's like riding a bike," she said, smirking. "Now if you're done playing in the water maybe we can go back to sleep. We've got work to do tomorrow."

"I like the sound of *we*," he said. "What changed?"

"I came to the realization that my life is in somewhat of a predicament." She shrugged. "It doesn't look like prison is on my Bingo card any longer. But dying by Taber's hands is still there, and that's not a square I'm looking to win."

"What else is on your Bingo card?" he asked curiously. The tension in the room skyrocketed and he moved closer, as if there were an invisible thread being tugged between them.

"Endless sexual tension and unsatisfied desire," she said cheekily.

He choked out a laugh. "You're something else, Evie."

Chapter Ten

The storm was still going strong two days later and Cal was going stir crazy. Or maybe it was just Evangeline who was driving him crazy. She hadn't been wrong about the endless sexual tension and unsatisfied desire. But their relationship was complicated. They had a history. Some good. Some not so good. But it was the future that was plaguing his dreams.

He was finding he very much wanted a future with Evie. The kind of future where they'd be lifelong partners—on the job and at home. They'd wasted too much time, though the years had given both of them the chance to grow up.

He was just now wrapping his own mind around the thought of marriage. It had been a disaster the first time, but it wasn't fair to even compare. He'd have given anything for Julie to listen to her parents and run the other direction from him. She'd still be alive if she'd listened. But Julie had been looking for a bad boy like in one of the romance novels she liked to read, and he'd been hell bent on destruction, looking for a way to keep the memories of Evangeline from creeping into his dreams. The marriage had been a disaster from the start.

He'd woken early and dressed for a workout. Sleeping next to Evangeline every night was unraveling his sanity and he needed to punch something. And just like the last three mornings, Evie had gotten out of bed and put her own workout gear on. And like clockwork she made her way to the kitchen because she didn't function without caffeine hitting her system.

By the time she was alert enough for them to make their way up to the gym, Cal was gritting his teeth and cursing himself for telling her that she was to stick to him like glue. The fumes from that glue were making him want to self-combust.

"Master of Puppets" blared from his phone, and he gave a sigh of relief, glad to have a distraction other than his own thoughts.

"Hold up a sec," he told Evie.

"Good," she said. "I'd rather have breakfast

anyway. I didn't get enough sleep last night. You're a restless sleeper."

He refrained from rolling his eyes. "Cruz," he said into the phone.

"We tapped into the FBI hotline and a tip came in early this morning," Atticus said. "A witness recognized Taber at a gas station in Atlanta and called it in."

"Uh-huh," Cal said. "Last I checked the reward is twenty-five thousand dollars. Witnesses start coming out of the woodwork. Everyone's grandpa becomes an assassin for the right price."

"Family loyalty is hard to come by," Atticus said dryly. "The only difference is this witness took a picture with his phone. Guess what Taber was driving?"

"A silver Mercedes?"

"Close enough," Atticus said. "A silver BMW rental from Hartsfield-Jackson Airport. Rented under the name Victor Timms."

Evie got out eggs from the fridge and a loaf of bread from the box. And then she gathered everything she needed to make French toast. It didn't look like they were making it to the gym anytime soon, so he made himself comfortable on one of the sleek barstools that lined the white marble island.

"I'm assuming his trip to Atlanta was successful?" Cal asked.

"We're not sure yet," Atticus said.

"Why do you sound worried about that?" Cal asked.

"Because Taber has never been one to hide his light under a bushel. We were expecting him to come to Atlanta since it's where Boulder Corp. is located. The FBI has had agents on Jenson Walker. His security has been briefed and beefed up."

"I hear a *but* in there somewhere."

"But he's gone missing, and we haven't found a body. Or any parts of a body."

"That is unusual," Cal said. "Maybe Jenson got spooked and decided to take off on his own."

"He would have to be a hell of a magician," Atticus said. "Security outside his office saw him shortly before eight o'clock. He was due in a board meeting at eight fifteen but never showed. No one was logged coming in or out of his office in that fifteen-minute timespan."

Cal grunted. "So where's Taber now?"

"We've adjusted satellite imagery to try and track him along the highway. We've taken control of the cameras at intersections and toll areas. We know he's heading east, so chances are Evangeline is next on his list. Nate and Eden should be there in the next few hours. And Max will take the red-eye so he can be there by morning. You'll have the backup you need."

Cal felt some of the pressure in his chest dissipate. Nate and Max. Warlock and Zeus in a former life. He knew he could trust them with his life, but more importantly he could trust them with Evie's life.

"Good to know. I'm about to crack open Boulder and DyniCorp. I've been cracking their digital safe for almost two days, but I should be well entrenched in the next hour or so. Both companies should feel good about their security. It's some of the best I've seen."

"I'm sure that will warm their hearts once they discover the breach," Atticus said.

"They're not going to discover the breach. I know how to cover my tracks."

"Or maybe it's a good idea, as a courtesy, to alert them they've got weak defenses."

"Eh," Cal said. "You're the one who has a moral compass about that kind of stuff. I'll leave it up to you."

Evie arched a brow at him and slid a plate in front of him. He winked at her and watched as she got fresh fruit, cream, and syrup and set it out neatly in front of their plates. She refilled her own coffee and took the seat next to his.

"What's your take on Boulder?" Cal asked. "Maybe I can track Walker once I breach the system."

"They're a billion-dollar company," Atticus said. "A competitive player in government contracts. Mostly aircraft for the military, but they dabble in a few other things. They've got restructuring problems. Charles Haywood was the CEO for more than twenty years, but he was diagnosed with Alzheimer's last year and has acted as CEO emeritus for the past six months so stockholders wouldn't get nervous at a change at the helm. Everyone loved Haywood. He's a good man."

"It's hard to be the guy that follows the guy," Cal said. "Is Haywood's diagnosis common knowledge?"

"They've kept a tight lid on it," Atticus said. "The board of directors hasn't even been officially notified, though most of them have to suspect. Haywood has always been good at making people feel at ease, even when things are about to hit the fan. He gave the standard speech about quality of life and wanting to slow down to spend time with his family, and that he fully supported Jenson Walker to take over as acting

CEO. But that he'd see the transition through for the first year."

"I take it people don't love Walker like they loved Haywood?" Cal asked, digging into the food in front of him.

"That's an understatement. Especially with Senator Biddle. Biddle and Charles Haywood go way back and they're friends. But like most things when the government is involved, money talks and personal favors are granted with the expectation that they'll be paid back when called in. And Biddle owed Charles Haywood a favor. It turns out Charles had a sound enough mind to call in the favor by asking Biddle to meet with Walker and give the contract to Boulder."

"Would Biddle have honored the favor?" Cal asked.

"Possibly. If there was no other way to get out of it. Haywood does still have some very lucid days, but I've heard through the grapevine they're becoming few and far between. Biddle probably hoped if he delayed long enough that Haywood wouldn't have known one way or the other."

Cal looked down at his plate and realized he'd eaten everything, and then he looked over at Evangeline. Her laptop was set up and it looked like she was getting caught up on work. His eyes started to glaze over watching her. He didn't know how she'd stood doing such boring work all these years.

He took his plate to the sink and then walked over to the area where he'd set up his computers. Ferreting out information on three top clearance companies, pulling video from behind the walls of Langley, and infiltrating different areas of the Pentagon took time and patience. Thankfully he had both. Both Boulder and DyniCorp had safeguards in place to recognize patterns and anomalies that appeared when someone was trying to hack the system. The program he'd written edged in a little bit at a time, so it was a continuous job of moving in and out without being detected.

He was close. Numbers and symbols were scrolling rapidly across the screen and his adrenaline surged.

"If Senator Biddle was planning to give the contract to Boulder because of his deal with Hayward, and the competition is getting knocked off, first with John Amir at AeroNaut and now with Jenson Walker missing, it kind of leaves the smoking gun pointing at DyniCorp."

"Believe me," Atticus said. "I'm aware. I've

been all over them like a rash. I've pulled all the financials for an audit and everyone associated is getting thoroughly investigated. Don't worry about DyniCorp. If they're involved in this in any way I'll light the match to burn them to the ground."

"I never doubted it for a second."

"Things will ramp up quick, Cal," Atticus said, his tone serious. "Taber doesn't like to delay his jobs. Don't let your guard down."

"No worries. And good call sending Nate. He owes me a hundred bucks. Convenient how he always happens to be out on assignment when I'm in town."

"He pays better bribes than you do," he said, and then hung up.

Evangeline had spent the past couple of days trying to figure out Cal's game. Which caused her to wonder why everything always had to be a game with them to begin with. Their time together had been pleasant—comfortable—and as familiar as their childhoods had been. It was making her nervous. Not to mention she was wondering when he was going to kiss her again.

She'd never stopped loving him. Even when she thought she'd hated him. And being forced together over the last couple of days had been an exercise in restraint. Especially when he looked at her the way he had been—those intense, longing looks that made her think he was going to swoop in and kiss her at any moment.

But he hadn't kissed her again. And God, how she'd wanted him to.

She'd been surprised how easily they'd moved into a steady routine. She was a private person by nature and treasured her solitude. She couldn't remember the last time she'd been in such close proximity to a person for multiple days.

But Cal somehow managed to stick close to her without invading her space. He just simply *was* in her space.

His conversation with Atticus had piqued her curiosity, but she'd learned from her father that if she looked like she wasn't paying attention than people tended to loosen their guard on what they said. So after she'd made breakfast she set up her laptop to get caught up on work. She'd been so far ahead on her projects that she could have taken a month off, and everything that was in her inbox she could've done with her eyes closed.

Cal hung up the phone and she could feel his eyes on her from behind.

"Thanks for breakfast," he said.

"We've all got to eat," she said dryly. "Though we're probably going to have to get groceries soon. I'd forgotten how much you eat. You were always a bottomless pit as a teenager. Looks like time hasn't changed much in that regard."

"At least Robert has a first-rate gym in this place," he said. "I normally just fuel to survive. But you're a good cook. Apparently all I needed to get my teenage appetite back was a good home-cooked meal."

"Hmm," she said as she swiveled on her barstool to face him.

"Looks like exciting work," he said, mouth twitching.

"Everyone needs a hobby," she said.

"Most people take up road cycling. Or knitting. Or read ridiculous amounts of romance novels."

She felt the warmth in her cheeks. If he'd wanted to come out and say that he'd been spying on her for the last ten years that was the easiest way to do it. One of the ways she stayed in shape was with road cycling. She loved the feel of the wind against her face as she soared downhill, and the way her thighs burned as she battled up a steep climb.

And knitting…well, she'd been bored and figured it was a good skill to learn. She hadn't mastered it and all she'd managed to create was a couple of lopsided blankets, but it had kept her hands occupied on nights when she'd been tempted to use them for other things, especially in those early months after everything had been taken from her.

As for the romance novels, it wasn't her fault that she was a fast reader. And what constituted a ridiculous amount? It's not like she lied about other plans to her co-workers whenever they invited her out for after-work drinks and instead went home to read a book in her bathtub and drink a glass of wine. At least…not always.

Instead of responding, she tightened her lips and cleared her dishes away, putting them in the dishwasher.

"That was Atticus on the phone," he said. "We're about to have some company."

"Atticus is coming here?" she asked, turning to face him, her embarrassment forgotten.

"Not Atticus," Cal said. "Nathan and Eden

Locke. Nate was part of our CIA black ops team."

"I've heard Dad talk about him," she said. "I've never met him though."

"He met Eden when Atticus sent him on a mission to track down a recruit that had been Israeli Mossad."

"Did he find the recruit?" she asked.

"He married her," Cal said, grinning. "She's a hell of an agent. I'm glad she's on our side."

"So what you're saying is that Atticus is kind of a black ops matchmaker."

Cal burst out with laughter, doubling over to catch his breath. "Oh, Atticus is going to love that one."

"Oh, God. Don't tell him I said that."

"I'll take full credit for it," he assured her. "Atticus never did have much of a sense of humor. He's a very serious kind of guy. But that doesn't mean the rest of us don't give him a jab from time to time, just to see if we can crack that shell."

"I'm sure it must give him a lot of peace to know he's running an agency of teenagers."

"As long as we get the job done," Cal said. "I want to go change before Nate and Eden get here. We won't have time to work out. Atticus said

Taber was spotted in Atlanta. They're using satellite imagery to try and track his route, but they know for sure he's headed east. You're the most likely target."

They headed back up the stairs to the bedroom they were sharing.

"Does that mean he found his target in Atlanta?" she asked.

"Don't know yet," Cal said, getting a fresh pair of jeans and a T-shirt from the closet. "No body has been found."

Evie looked down at her oversized shirt and leggings and wondered if she could get away with wearing them for the rest of the day, but she figured it was probably a good idea to make a good impression on the people sent to protect her with their lives.

So she grabbed her own jeans and debated over the folded clothes she'd rescued from her room down the hall. It had been a long time since she'd paid attention to her clothes. Hiding her body had seemed fitting with having to hide her true identity. But she'd felt something surge through her the day before when she'd sat behind Cal's console and felt the magic run through the tip of her fingers.

Now that she'd had the taste she knew she

couldn't go back to the woman she'd pretended to be for the last decade. Even if Cal asked her to.

She grabbed a black tank top from the pile and her jeans. It was still warm and they were in Florida and the humidity was thick. But she was her father's daughter. Be prepared in all things. So she chose jeans instead of shorts, grabbed sneakers and socks, and went into the bathroom to change. She rolled her eyes at Cal, who didn't seem to have any problem with stripping down in front of her.

He was dressed when she came back out, his gun in the holster at his waist and an extra magazine in his pocket. He wore a lightweight Gore-Tex jacket with pockets that probably had any number of weapons hidden inside.

His brow arched when he noticed she wore a tank top instead of an oversized ugly shirt, and she felt a tingle of excitement as his eyes darkened. She went to the nightstand and grabbed her .9mm to keep on hand. She could tell something had shifted in Cal, and it put her own senses on high alert.

Cal's phone rang just as they were coming back downstairs.

"This is Cruz," he said. And then, "Send them to the house."

"They're here?" she asked. "That was fast."

"They were scheduled to come in today no matter what," Cal told her. "They just got back from a mission a couple of days ago and had time to debrief and decompress."

Cal opened the large glass front door and they watched a gray SUV come through the gate and down the long drive of palms, circling the fountain before coming to a stop.

One of the most beautiful women she'd ever seen got out of the passenger side. Her dark hair was pulled back from a strikingly exotic face, and though she was slender, the muscles in her shoulders and arms were clearly defined in the spaghetti strap tank she wore. Evie's brows knitted together when the woman came close enough for her to see the three puckered scars high up on her chest.

Evie knew by looking at them they were gunshot wounds, and by the placement of them, she was lucky to be alive at all.

"Eden," Cal said, pulling her into a hug. "Beautiful as ever. I can't believe you married this dunderhead. Did you know he once went an entire mission only eating Vienna sausages? He kept trying to convince the rest of us it was why he had so much energy."

"They say love is blind," she said, laughing. And then she looked at Evie. "You must be Evangeline. I've heard so much about you."

"Call me Evie," she said, liking the woman instantly.

"Don't y'all stand there and act like I'm the hired help," Nate said, opening the trunk to grab their bags.

"Oh, didn't see you there, Warlock," Cal said. "You look different. I think you might be putting on some weight around the middle. I hear married life does that to a man."

Eden and Evie laughed, and Evie thought Nate looked like he was in the best shape of his life. There wasn't an ounce of fat on him anywhere. She'd grown up around men who had certain skill sets, and she'd learned to recognize them at an early age. They all moved the same, and there was something in their eyes that brought an initial wariness to anyone they came in contact with. Though Nate was a more presentable first impression than Cal could ever hope to be. Most people walked in the opposite direction whenever they saw Cal coming. Maybe it was the tattoos.

But Nathan Locke was Cal's complete opposite. She'd never seen anyone whose description fit *California* better than his. He was a couple of inches taller than Cal, and his white-blond hair was long enough to be casually tousled around his angular face. A short beard a shade darker than what was on his head covered his cheeks. She'd expected to see blue or green eyes with his coloring, but when he took off his sunglasses she could see they were so dark they were almost black.

"I will kill you, Cyph," Nate said, hanging his sunglasses in the front of his shirt. "Now come get some of these bags. We brought an arsenal. Eden doesn't like to leave home without them. I guess some women don't like to leave home without their purses. For Eden it's guns."

"My kind of woman," Cal said.

"So you're Lockwood's daughter," Nate said, looking back and forth between her and Cal.

"That's what they tell me," Evie said. "I can't prove it though."

"You certainly don't look like him. Thank God for small blessings. Now I see why Cal has been so protective of you all these years."

Evie arched a brow. "Oh really? In what way?"

Nate cleared his throat and grinned. "You know, like telling anyone he came in contact with that he'd kill them if they so much as looked in your direction. That kind of stuff."

Cal growled low in his throat and Nate laughed. Thunder rumbled overhead as clouds moved in.

"I thought Florida was supposed to be sunny," Nate said. "It's done nothing but rain since we got here. Next time you witness a murder let's rendezvous in Italy."

Evie grinned, liking him immediately.

"I see you met my wife," Nate said. "Don't play poker with her. She counts cards."

"Don't worry," Evie said. "So do I. It makes things more interesting."

"My kind of woman," Eden said.

It was obvious the couple loved each other very much. They almost looked like normal people, but they were highly trained agents and never to be underestimated.

She wondered what it would be like to have a partner like that in every sense of the word—in marriage and in work. It obviously suited them both because their thoughts and actions were in sync as they all walked around the perimeter of the house before the rain started again, cataloguing entrance and exit points and looking for signs of weakness.

"We'll try not to invade your privacy too much," Eden said. "We're just here to be an extra set of eyes. Which is going to be interesting if the rain comes in hard again. It provides an excellent cover for someone wanting to get close to the house. How's the security system?"

"It's crap," Cal said.

"Geez, tell us how you really feel, Cal," Evie said.

"Just telling the truth, sugar. Your dad didn't have the kind of security in mind that we need when he bought the place for your mom, and he never upgraded after she died since he's rarely here. It has a standard alarm system and exterior cameras. But they've been spotty at best since the rain started. The wind knocks them out of alignment, and it's a pain in the ass to go out and move them back into place. Basically, we're working blind except for the lookout agents.

"Ahh, to be a peon again and get all the exciting assignments," Nate said with a grin. "Those were the days."

"I wouldn't know," Cal said, his mouth quirked in good humor. "I was never a peon."

The storm intensified over the next several hours, and the sky had darkened. Cal was getting antsy, and he kept getting up from the table where he'd been working to check the windows and doors.

"You're driving me crazy, Cyph," Nate said, playing cards with Eden and Evie at the table. "You never did learn patience."

"He's close," Cal said. "I can feel it."

Cal's cell phone rang. He didn't recognize the number, but that wasn't uncommon. Agents used burner cells most of the time.

"Cruz," he said.

"Sir, this is Agent James. My partner and I are at a little restaurant called Rosa's. We've been staked out here to watch cars as they cross the bridge. We were about to call in a silver BMW when the car turned into the lot and Taber walked into the restaurant. He's got a corner table with his back to the wall. Do you want us to detain him?"

"You and your partner hang tight," Cal said. "I'll be there in a few minutes. Don't take your eyes off him."

"Yes, sir."

Cal disconnected and looked at Nate. "Taber is at a restaurant called Rosa's. It's about a ten-minute drive from here."

Nate looked hesitant. "Do you think it's legitimate?"

"I think it's worth checking out," Cal said. "Atticus said this island is crawling with agents. I have no idea where they're stationed or who they are. But he mentioned the BMW. That's fairly new information that Atticus would have relayed to the rest of the team so they could keep an eye out."

Eden looked at Nate and said, "You and Cal go. I'll stay here with Evie. If something's wrong give us a heads-up and we'll go to plan B and get her moved to safety until you get back."

"I'll alert the agents next door to move in closer." Nate opened his duffle bag and pulled out an extra magazine to stick in his pocket and then he grabbed a sheathed knife and strapped it to his ankle.

Evie didn't know why the separation made her so anxious. She'd gotten used to having Cal as her primary protector. And it wasn't that she didn't think Eden could do a good job. She was just… different.

Eden had walked Nate to the door and they were saying their goodbyes, and Cal felt a pang of envy for what they had.

He held out his hand to Evie and she put her

hand in his tentatively. And then he pulled her to her feet.

"You going to be okay?" he asked. "You look nervous."

"I'm fine," she said. "I'll just be glad when this is over."

"Evie," he said. He couldn't seem to look away. She was so beautiful. "When this is over…"

"Yes?" she asked.

"I think we have some things to talk about when this is over."

"Cal," she whispered.

Before he could help himself he leaned in and kissed her, pulling her into his arms and wishing he didn't have to let her go. He pulled away and then gave her another kiss on her forehead.

"Don't take any chances," he said, warning her. "I know you can protect yourself. But let Eden do her job."

"We'll be fine," she said. "Just get him and finish the job so you can get back and we can have that conversation. I was thinking maybe we could have it at a place where Atticus or my father can't interrupt us. I wouldn't mind disappearing for a while."

"I think I can manage that," he said, and kissed her again.

He went to meet Nate at the door and pulled up the center cushion of the couch along the way, grabbing the extra weapon hidden there along with another magazine.

"Hit the panic button on your phone if you need us," Cal said.

And then they were gone.

Chapter Eleven

"So she's the one, huh?" Nate asked.

The windshield wipers were working overtime and the edges of the streets were full of water, so it spewed up the side of the SUV as they sped down the road. Visibility wasn't great, and Nate slammed on his brakes at the last second when he realized the stoplight was red.

"She's always been the one," Cal said. "Things were just complicated."

"I figured as much," Nate said quietly. "You know we all knew something went down on that mission in Russia. Atticus did a little digging when you went a little nuts and cut your comm units. It didn't take him long to put the pieces together that Evie was the Black Lily and who we were looking for."

Cal blew out a breath, trying to release the tightness in his chest. "Why didn't anyone ever say anything?"

"To protect you and Evie," Nate said. "And to keep Lockwood from finding out. I don't think he would have handled it well, and it seemed like you had everything well in hand. I think Lockwood would have seen it as a betrayal and how he responded might have set her on a darker path. You did the right thing for her, Cal."

"Yeah, well it hasn't always felt like it. And she hasn't always thought so."

"She was just a kid," Nate said. "But I see the way she looks at you. Whatever happened between y'all in Russia has been forgiven."

"Now I just have to convince Atticus to give her a job. And if he knows the truth about her that might not be an easy task."

"Probably easier than you think," Nate said. "Atticus has been keeping tabs on her all these years just like you have. He knows her skills, and you know how he is. He'd hire her in a heartbeat just to keep her from going to the competition."

"Evie called Atticus a black ops matchmaker," Cal said. "I'm starting to think she might be right because you know I'm going to have to marry her.

And it was Atticus that forced me to take this assignment."

"Please let me hear you call him that to his face," Nate said, laughing. "No mission could be more exciting than his reaction."

Evie shuffled the cards and then dealt another round. It made things a lot more interesting when both players cheated. And cheated well.

Eden's phone rang and she answered automatically. "Locke," she said.

"This is Agent James again. Agent Locke and Cruz just arrived and reassigned us to the house. We're to be your backup. Our ETA is about two minutes. He said you'll need to let us in through the gate."

"Roger that, James. See you in two minutes."

"As long as I can get out of this blasted rain I'm up for anything," James said.

She laughed. "You might need a canoe to get to the front door, but I promise it's dry inside."

"Are they finished already?" Evie asked after Eden had hung up.

"Replacement agents are on the way." Eden put her cards facedown on the table and got to her feet. Her gun had been sitting on the table next to her phone, so she picked it up and held it down at her side.

"Don't tell your father this, but all this glass is stupid," Eden said. "What good is a glass front door?"

"Your secret is safe with me," Evie said.

"Stand behind this wall here while I buzz them through the gate," she said. "We don't want to give anyone a clear shot at you, just in case."

"Just in case is fine with me." Evie followed her to the front door and stood behind the entry wall.

The intercom by the front door buzzed and Eden answered the call.

"This is the front gate," a voice said. "I've got an Agent James and Agent Carter here. Identifications check out."

"Let them through," Eden said. "Alert the agents next door of the shift change."

"Yes, ma'am," the guard said.

"It's hard to see anything out there," Eden said, turning off the lights in the entryway so she could see better. But the rain was heavy and they could barely see the sedan as it made its way down the drive. "They're pulling under the portico at the side. Big mistake. They should've pulled right in front of the door. They'll be soaked to the skin."

Evie peeked around the wall and watched as two dark figures in raincoats and hoods ran toward the cover of the front of the house.

"Company men," Eden said. "Looks like FBI standard issue. They're not known for being fun, but maybe we can beat them at cards."

Eden's gun was in her right hand and she moved to open the front door with her left. Evie's gut was screaming a warning the closer they got, and she saw how foolish the glass front door was, despite its beauty.

She was about to yell a warning when a shot rang and a hole appeared in the center of the tempered glass. Eden stumbled back and fired off several shots and one of the men went down.

Evangeline turned the deadbolts, knowing it wouldn't hold the other man off for long, and then she hit the alarm on her phone.

"Eden," she said, looking at the blood that soaked the woman's shirt.

"I'm fine, I'm fine." Eden rolled to her hands and knees and stumbled to her feet. "Get moving. Go to plan B. Move!"

Evie grabbed Eden around the waist, leaving her gun hand free, and they took off for the back of the house and the beach. All she could do was pray for the rain to come harder, so visibility was difficult. Of course, that was a two-edged sword. They wouldn't be able to see Taber either. At least, she assumed it was Taber. She hadn't gotten a good look at his face.

"Who was the other guy?" Evie asked, her breath coming in shallow pants. "I thought Taber worked alone?"

"He does. He either paid someone to knock on the door so we wouldn't be suspicious, or he's taken on a partner for this job.

"I didn't recognize the man you shot and the other guy had his raincoat pulled up, so I didn't see his face."

"We've got to make it to the cove," Eden said. "Unless Taber knows specifically where it is he'll never find it. We'll be at our weakest when we go out those doors and are exposed on the beach. I'm hoping the rain will give us enough cover."

They made it out the sliding glass door at the back of the house in time to hear gunshots shatter the kitchen windows.

"Go! Go!" Eden said. "Stay hunched over and low. Make yourself a smaller target."

The storm slapped at them angrily, soaking them to the skin in an instant. Evie tightened her grip around Eden's waist when the woman stumbled, and she was worried about the amount of blood she'd lost. The wound was in the upper shoulder, but she needed to get pressure on it soon.

It was impossible to hear anything other than the rumble of the storm and her own heartbeat. And it seemed like an impossibly long way to the outcropping of rocks. But she followed Eden's instructions and they stayed low, moving into the wind. When she checked to see if anyone was behind them she could barely see past the length of her own arm. She just had to pray there was no one there. And if there was someone there, that he couldn't see her.

Eden stumbled again and went to her knees this time. "Keep going," she said. "I'll be right behind you."

Evie knelt down next to her and stripped off the tank top she wore, leaving her in nothing but her bra, but she figured it was no different than a bathing suit and life-or-death situations weren't the time to be modest. Wet fabric wasn't easy to work with, but she was at least able to put pressure on the wound. They stopped long enough for Evie to tie it around her shoulder and then she helped Eden get to her feet again.

"We're almost there," Evie said. "Keep moving."

"Nate is going to be so pissed. He doesn't like it when I get shot."

"Better shot than dead."

"Good point."

Thank God for bad weather.

When the panic alarm sounded they were only halfway to the restaurant, despite the fact that well over ten minutes had passed.

The sound was loud and shrill and Nate didn't hesitate. He spun the wheel and did a U-turn in the middle of an intersection. He pressed the pedal to the floor and sped back to the house.

They were both on their phones trying to contact Eden and Evie.

"No answer," Nate said, banging his fist on the dashboard.

"The alarm sounds to all the agents in the area," Cal said. "They'll be setting up a perimeter to keep him from leaving."

Cal couldn't remember time stretching the way it did in the moments between when the alarm sounded and when they screeched to a stop outside the gates of the mansion.

"Look there," Cal said, pointing to the two security guards that lay facedown in the water.

"The gate's jammed open," Nate said. "For an easy getaway. He wouldn't want to get trapped."

"That's a good sign." Cal took a breath of relief and tried to convince himself that everything was going to be all right. "It means he's still here somewhere."

Nate parked the SUV halfway down the drive, and they were both out with their weapons at the ready as they ran the rest of the way to the front of the house, using the palm trees for cover.

"Look there," Nate said.

"Silver BMW," Cal said, looking at the car parked under the side portico. "That takes some brass. He drove it right to the front of the house."

"It would've been hard to see with the rain like it is," Nate said. "But the good news is he's either dead or he's still here. I'll disable the car."

Once the BMW was missing a fuse to keep it from starting they made their way to the front door and the man who lay prone on the ground. He lay on his back, staring straight up, and there was a bullet hole in his throat and another in the chest.

"Eden's work," Nate said. "That's not Taber. Who is it?"

Cal recognized the man's face from the files he'd been poring over the last three days. "That's Jenson Walker. Former CEO of Boulder Corp. I guess we know who was behind the hit in the first place. Let's go. Taber is still unaccounted for. He got a shot off. There's blood on the floor."

"God," Nate said.

They tried the door but it was bolted from the inside. So they ran back to the SUV and headed around the side of the house.

"Where are the freaking agents?" Cal said, his finger tapping on the side of his weapon. "This place should be swarming."

"The closest neighbor is a mile down the road and they're all crammed in that guesthouse because of the weather. They should be pulling up any minute."

"Useless," Cal said. "And stupid of us to be tricked into leaving. How'd he get my number?"

"They've probably got the house wired or intercepted one of your previous calls. There are any number of ways to get unlisted numbers. Nothing is private with technology. I'm going to be really pissed if Eden got shot again. That woman is going to be the death of me."

Cal watched his friend as he sped toward the beach. His words and tone were calm, but his knuckles were white as he gripped the wheel and the pulse in the side of his throat was beating rapidly. They were both soaked to the skin, but the iciness of the rain was barely felt through the heat of their adrenaline.

"It doesn't matter how many missions we go on," Nate said. "The fear of losing her is real. I don't know how Atticus is coping. I'm not sure what I'd do if anything ever happened to Eden."

The wind rocked the car back and forth, and the wipers were fighting a losing battle. The off-road tires gripped the wet sand as they sped along the beach as far as they could before the rocks blocked them.

"Why was Jenson Walker here with Taber?" Nate asked. "We've got loads of intel on Taber and he's never taken on a partner before."

"He's never had a target guarded by trained operatives inside a compound," Cal said. "He had to make some adjustments so he could get the job done. Taber is a user. Which is why Walker is dead by the front door and Taber is still alive."

"I can't see anything," Nate said, coming to a stop. "He could be right on top of us. We need to move faster. I don't have a good feeling in my gut. Something is wrong."

"Leave me here," Eden said weakly. "I can wedge myself on the other side of that larger rock there. He'll never see me."

"You'll be in the water," Evie said. "Some of those waves will go over your head." Evangeline was worried. Really worried. Eden's color wasn't good and she was going in and out of consciousness. "The rocks are smoother closer to the lagoon. You can't stay here, so our only option is up. Get on my back."

Eden tried to laugh but she didn't have the energy. "I'm a good five inches taller than you. That's not going to work."

"Up and at 'em, Debbie Downer." Evie kept watch on the horizon, looking for Taber to appear like mist right in front of them. "You're not going to quit on my watch. If we can make it up to that ledge then I think we'll be hidden well enough without having to go down into the lagoon."

Eden nodded, but Evie could tell even that was a chore. "Just give me a boost." So Evie pulled her to her feet and steadied her.

Evie laced her fingers and braced herself for Eden's weight. She didn't think the other woman would have the upper body strength to pull herself up on the rocks, but Eden dug in and gathered resolve from somewhere because her fingers bit into the rocks and the muscles in her arms flexed as she pulled herself up.

"You got it," Evie encouraged, praying her wound wouldn't start bleeding badly again. Eden had already lost so much blood.

Salt spray stung Evie's eyes and wet ropes of hair felt like whips against her face as she climbed up behind Eden. The other woman half crawled, half dragged herself the rest of the way to the rougher rocks toward the top that hadn't been worn smooth from crashing waves.

Evie had to give it to her, she wasn't sure she'd have been able to keep going if she'd been in a similar situation. When they got to the top Evie wedged Eden between two large rocks. They couldn't get any wetter, but the cold was starting to set in and Eden's teeth were chattering. Her color had a gray tinge to it, and Evie could see her visibly trying to get control of her breathing.

"Don't worry about me," Eden said. "I've been here before. But I'm pretty close to passing out so I'm not going to be much use to you."

Evie nodded and tightened the makeshift bandage as best as she could. The bullet was still inside Eden, and she didn't know if that was a good thing or a bad thing. There was no telling the kind of damage the bullet was doing inside. On the other hand, an exit wound would have made slowing the bleeding infinitely harder.

"Take this," Eden said, handing her the extra Glock. "Cal and Nate will be here soon. They'd see what happened at the house and go directly to plan B. You shouldn't have to wait long. Nate is going to be frantic. Tell him I told you I'm going to be okay."

And with that, Eden slowly faded out of consciousness, until her head slumped to the side and rested against the rocks.

Evie put two fingers against Eden's neck, just to make sure there was still a pulse, and she let out a breath of relief when she found it.

"Everything is going to be fine." She stood up and fumbled for the phone in her pocket to see if she had service, and that's when the bullet ricocheted off the rock next to her.

She lost her footing and tumbled back down the rocks to the sand, scraping her knees and elbows along the way. The gun fell from her grasp and landed in the sand a few feet away. The phone went in the other direction. She scrambled for the gun just as another bullet hit the rocks.

He must have gotten a glimpse of her when she'd stood up, but she didn't think he could see where she'd landed. She looked around, trying to get a glimpse of him, but she couldn't tell what direction the shots were coming from. The rain made it hard to see and to hear. Another shot hit the rocks, this one closer to the shore where she was. And then there was another higher up. His shots were wild, and she figured he was probably trying to get her to run. But the only place to run was back to the house and toward Taber. It was impossible to climb back up the rocks and then down the other side. Not without really hurting herself. That would have been a tenuous climb in perfect weather.

She kept low and shielded by the rocks. The weight of the gun in her hand felt good and familiar. He wanted her to move. To run. So she'd just wait him out. The key to survival was to not panic. She needed to think like her father had taught her to think.

She was a target. And she was just another job for Taber. Plain and simple. It wasn't personal. She'd just happened to be the unlucky person who could identify him and link him to Senator

Biddle's murder. In her mind she knew it wasn't personal. But it sure as hell felt personal.

The next gunshot made her jump slightly, and then it was followed by a steady stream of gunfire. Pieces of rock flew in all directions, and she felt the sting as one of them sliced her cheek. She hoped to God Eden was hidden well enough so she didn't get caught in the crossfire.

Evie knew her options and time were up. He was moving closer, continuing to fire and then reloading his magazine. He'd eventually be right on top of her and then she'd be at a disadvantage. She could either sit there and wait for him to kill her with a lucky shot, or she could fire back in the general direction she thought the bullets were coming from.

Another bullet hit the rocks about ten feet over her head and she took a last deep breath and started firing. She immediately started moving at a fast pace, and she said every prayer she knew along the way, looking for the next place she could take cover.

She didn't know if it was an act of God or good luck, she wasn't one to question, but the rain slowed and the fog cleared just enough—a split second of time—for Taber's silhouette to be visible. She didn't hesitate to pull the trigger. There was no second-guessing in a life-or-death situation. And she kept pulling the trigger until the magazine was empty.

As fast as it stopped, the rain started again with a fierce gust of wind, the fog rolling off the ocean and onto the shore. Her heart pounded and the rain and salt stung her eyes. Her flesh was pebbled with cold and she only wore her bra and jeans. Her shoes had protected her feet from the rocks, but her body was scraped and bleeding in several places. She was starting to feel the pain. She wasn't exactly at her best. But she was alive. And that counted for something.

Only seconds later Cal and Nate were climbing over the first rock barrier and they were staring between her and Taber's body in wide-eyed shock.

"God, Evie," Cal said, stripping out of his jacket and wrapping it around her. "You're a mess." And then he pulled her in his arms and she buried her face in his neck. He was real. And she was real. And she was alive.

"Eden," Nate yelled. "Where is she?"

"The rocks at the top of the lagoon," Evie said. "She needs help. She's been shot. I'll take you there." She pulled back from Cal and then started the climb again, ignoring Taber's body.

And then she led them to the place where she left Eden, finding her still slumped between the rocks.

"She took one in the shoulder and lost some blood," she told Nate.

Nate climbed the rocks with ease and was next to Eden in moments, feeling for the pulse in her neck.

"She told me to tell you that she's going to be fine," Evie said.

Nate nodded and checked beneath the makeshift bandage, looking at the wound. "She's been trained to withstand trauma to her body. But it's not a practice that should get too much use in a person's lifetime."

"Do you need help getting her down?" Cal asked.

"I'll carry her down and hand her off to you at the bottom, and then I'm going to get her to the hospital. The bleeding has turned sluggish and her pulse is strong, but she's going to need a couple pints. And the bullet is still in there from what I can tell. I didn't find an exit wound."

Nate lifted Eden and climbed down as best he could with her tucked under one arm, and when he reached the lowest ledge he handed her gently down to Cal. They got her loaded in the SUV,

Nate saluted them goodbye, and then they sped away.

There were lights everywhere around the house, and flashing lights and cars seemed to be coming in from all directions.

"She'll be okay?" Evie asked as they made their way back toward the house and the chaos ensuing there. She couldn't wait to get out of the rain. In fact, she would be okay if she never saw rain again.

"She'll be fine," Cal said. "Eden's tough. She's been through worse than this."

Her legs were shaking uncontrollably by the time they waded through wet sand to the long, bricked walkway back toward the house. When they reached the pool she sat down hard on one of the loungers under a cabana, so she could at least get out of the rain.

Cal sat next to her and pulled her into his lap.

"Sorry," she said. "I just needed to sit down a second. I'm not sure I can put one foot in front of the other."

"EMTs are on the way to check you out," he said. "Some of those scratches look deep. You might need some stitches."

"I'm fine," she said. "Nothing a hot shower and a couple of Band-Aids won't fix."

"You scared the hell out of me," Cal said. "The closer we got, all I could hear was gunfire. It sounded like a war zone."

"It felt like one." She laid her head against his shoulder and he held her while her body processed the adrenaline and her shaking subsided. "I need to tell you something."

"I need to tell you something too," he said.

"I need to go first."

"Okay."

"I grew up loving you," she said. "From the time I was eight years old I could never see myself loving anyone but you. I couldn't even dream of myself growing old with anyone but you. And then for a time I told myself I hated you. I told myself you were rejecting the real me, who I was meant to be. So I told myself I would never love a man who couldn't accept the real me. I told myself I hated you."

"Evie," he said, and she could hear the anguish in his voice.

"But I know that you were protecting me. And telling myself I hated you and actually hating you are two different things. It's hard to destroy that childhood love. I think it must be the strongest thing in the world. I thought my heart would shatter the day I found out you got married. In every girlish fantasy I'd ever had, it was always me standing next to you in white."

"It should have been," Cal said softly. "We've both made mistakes. It's what we do going forward that matters."

"I know," she said. "Which is why I need you to know that I forgive you. And I never stopped loving you."

"Thank God," he said. "Because I was prepared to do whatever I needed to convince you. I love you. Everything about you. Including that twenty-year-old girl who was starved for attention. If I'd been another kind of man I would have taken you with me and we'd have wreaked havoc on the whole world."

"But you're not another kind of man," she said. "You're a good man. One of the best. And I love you more because of it."

"I have a proposal to make," he said.

Evie gasped and her head jerked up in surprise.

"No, not that kind of proposal," Cal said, grinning. "At least not yet. This isn't the time or the place. Though I'm wanting to know if that gasp was good or bad. You seemed a little taken off guard."

"What's your proposal?" she asked, shaking her head.

"I'm willing to bet that your father and Atticus are on the way as we speak," he said.

Evie groaned, dropping her head to his shoulder. "I don't think I can face my father right now. I love him. And I know he loves me in his way. But I'm not up to confronting him about the choices he made. And I'm not up for the argument that is going to happen when he finds out you're making nefarious proposals to his daughter."

"Hey, you don't even know what the proposal is yet," he said. "How do you know it's nefarious?"

"Because I know you," she said, smiling slightly.

"Fine," he said. "It's nefarious. Why don't we get in the car and go? Right now. I've got a safe house about twenty miles from here where we can stop and clean up. And then I've got a catamaran in the Charleston harbor that I haven't gotten to sail near enough."

"I'd need to pack," she said. "There's no way we can disappear before my father gets here."

He stood up and helped her to her feet. "I'm a determined man with a nefarious proposal. I can do anything I set my mind to. We'll pick up clothes along the way. All you're going to need is a bathing suit anyway."

She snorted out a laugh and followed him through the shadows. "I'm sure that's not all I'll need. Where will we go? How will we get out of here?"

"You ask a lot of questions," he said. "Where's your spontaneity?"

"I'm more of a planner."

"Ahh, I hear there's one in every couple," he said. "Good thing you're with me so you can loosen up some. As for your questions, I was thinking Australia. And as for getting out of here, we're going to get in my car and I'm going to tell everyone I'm taking you to the hospital."

"Sounds like you've thought of everything," she said. "It just so happens I've got some time off, and I've never been to Australia. But you know they'll find us."

"Maybe so, but they'll leave us in peace. At least for a while."

He opened the garage bay and took the keys from the hook on the wall inside before opening the passenger door for Evie. Then he got behind the wheel and started the car, drawing looks from a couple of the agents that were combing the grounds.

"Why will they leave us in peace?" she asked.

"Because Atticus knows when to pick his battles where his agents are concerned. He was my team leader for a long time. He'll keep your father at bay. But we'll eventually have to face him."

"Eventually," she said with a sigh. "But maybe we can wait until we have a couple of kids first. That ought to get him used to the idea of you seducing his daughter and dragging her halfway across the world."

He laughed and drove out of the garage and toward the front gate that had been left open for Taber's escape. A couple of agents tried to flag him down, but he'd never answered to the FBI and he wasn't going to start now.

"It sounds like you've got a nefarious proposal of your own," he said.

She grinned and winked at him. "Baby, you have no idea."

The next book in the Dynamis Security Series, *A Concerto of Crows and Cowards*, hits stores in Summer of 2024. Here's a sneak peek!

Five Years Ago…

"I'm pregnant."

Jade Jax stared at herself in the mirror—wide green eyes tinged with a hint of shock and panic. She knew if she didn't practice saying the words aloud, she'd never get them out when it was time to do it for real. So much for birth control.

Nausea rolled through her and she gritted her teeth and breathed out slowly, trying to delay the inevitable. Her face was pale and clammy, and she'd become good friends with the end stall in the ladies' room in the Department of Justice building over the past three weeks.

"Dammit." She raced into the stall and emptied what was left in her stomach. It was only vaguely annoying she'd been in there often enough to notice one of the floor tiles was cracked in the shape of the Virgin Mary. Mostly it just reminded her she needed to pray. Then maybe she could put something in her stomach without it reappearing again.

She stumbled back to the sink and splashed cold water onto her face, and then she wetted a few paper towels and let the cold trickle down the middle of her breasts. She had to pull herself together. There were less than two hours until go time. The next mission was an important one, and Max would detain her and make her stay stateside if he thought she was sick—even if it was her own husband who was the mission.

Donovan Jax had been in deep cover inside Alexander Ramos's organization for the last eighteen months. It was a dangerous job—a job she'd begged him not to take. They'd fought over it for weeks, but in the end she'd lost the battle. Donovan felt he was the right man for the job—the only person who could infiltrate the organization and pass on vital information to the DEA. And the hard part was accepting he was right. He was a good man, a good agent, and justice would always be more important than his safety. Falling in love with a hero was hell.

Their time together over the last year and a half had been sparse—stolen weekends in remote locations where they hadn't wasted time talking but instead had fallen straight into bed. When the time was added up, they'd actually been apart longer than they'd been married. It had been four weeks since she'd seen him last—four weeks since they'd made love. And made a baby.

Her hand went to her stomach protectively. Maybe this baby was a sign. She and the rest of the team were flying down to extract Donovan from Mexico. The assignment had gotten too dangerous, and Ramos was beginning to suspect some of his top men of betraying him. More than one body of his known lieutenants had been found—at least what had been left of them.

Don't think about it. He's coming home.

The DEA had enough information to begin the process of ending Ramos's reign forever. Donovan would come home, and they could be a family without threats or danger hanging over their heads at every turn. In fact, maybe it was time to turn in her badge and her weapon. The past ten years felt more like fifty, and the weight of the world was getting awfully heavy—not to mention the rifle she had to use much too frequently.

The more she thought about it, the more she knew it was the right decision. Max would throw a fit, but he could find another agent to replace her. The child growing inside of her couldn't grow up without a mother if anything happened to her.

Excerpt of Concerto of Crows and Cowards

Jade patted her face dry with a towel and slapped her cheeks for a little color. She had a mission to prepare for, and it was the most important mission of her life. Donovan was coming home.

"I'm pregnant," she said one last time to the mirror. This time she couldn't help but smile.

———

The DEA offices were on the fifth floor of the Department of Justice building, and she headed down the long gray corridor to her small office. They were supposed to meet at 14:30 for a briefing before the plane took off. She had just enough time to change clothes and check her weapons one final time.

Her office was a small square dominated by a metal desk. The floors were gray industrial grade carpet and the walls were stark white. A bookshelf stood in the corner, and the shelves bowed under the weight of books—anything from non-fiction to thrillers to the romances she kept on the bottom shelf so the guys wouldn't give her a hard time. She spent more time at work than home anyway, so it made sense to have the things she enjoyed close by. A green plant flourished on the

Excerpt of Concerto of Crows and Cowards

corner of her desk, and pictures sat on every free surface. It was a cramped and overflowing space, but she wouldn't trade it for anything. It was hers. And having things that belonged solely to her was something she'd learned to treasure.

Jade pulled her pack from the bottom drawer of her desk and changed into black cargo pants and a long sleeved black T-shirt. She pulled the pins from her hair and let it fall around her shoulders, brushing it out quickly before pulling it back in a ponytail. Maybe it was time to cut it short. She wouldn't want to deal with the hassle of long hair when the baby was born.

Jade checked the magazine in her Sig and pocketed another two, but her pride and joy was in the long black case under her desk. She pulled it out and set it on top of her desk, flicking open the locks with her thumbs and pushing back the lid. The M-40A3 rifle gleamed back at her—the black so smooth and polished she could see her reflection in it.

The knock on her door had her yelling out, "Enter," and she closed the lid on the case with a snap.

She knew something was wrong the moment Max stepped inside and closed the door behind him. Max was a good boss and a great agent, and she knew his responsibility weighed heavily on him. He truly cared about his agents, and he'd flip his middle finger to the bureaucrats and politicians if it meant those under his command were going to get screwed. There weren't many she'd trust to watch her back if things went to hell, but he was one of them.

But the Max she'd worked with the last few years was almost unrecognizable in the man who stood before her. His face was drawn and his eyes shadowed with grief. His hair was disheveled as if he'd been running his fingers through it, and his normally impeccable clothes were wrinkled—his tie shoved in his pocket and the collar of his shirt unbuttoned.

"What's wrong?" Her voice was foreign to her ears. Her palms slicked with sweat and her lungs felt as if they were bursting in her chest. Somewhere deep inside she knew—knew that whatever Max had to say would break her.

She wiped her palms on her pants and shook her head, coming around the desk to face him head on.

"Jade," he said. And she knew. She knew Donovan was dead, as if someone had flicked a switch off inside of her.

"No, you're wrong." Her soul was splintering

into pieces and he expected her to just believe him, without proof. "You'll see. We can leave early and go get him. We'll do the extraction and you'll see he's okay. We'll bring him home." Her voice rose higher and higher as panic took over. She was trained to never panic—to breathe deep and keep her focus. But she couldn't do it this time. She just couldn't.

"I'm sorry, Jade." Max reached out for her, but she moved back, knocking the picture frame from her desk to the floor. Glass crunched beneath her feet, and she bent down to salvage what was left of her wedding photo.

Glass sliced at her finger and blood welled instantly, but she pulled the picture from the shards and held it against her breast.

"No," she said again. "No, no, no. It's just a misunderstanding. I want to talk to our contacts in Mexico. I want someone to go in and bring him out now. If he's in danger, then we don't need to waste a minute."

Max knelt down beside her and held her trembling hands. The blood from the cut on her finger welled faster, soaking into the white cuff of his shirt.

"He's gone, Jade." His voice cracked, and he had to swallow a couple of times before he could go on. "I've spent the last three hours trying to cut through red tape and lies to get the answers I needed. Let me get this out," he said. "You know I have to say the words."

She shook her head, but it didn't stop him from speaking. "I'm sorry for your loss. Donovan Jax was killed in the line of duty."

"I said no!" she screamed. Her fist connected with the side of his face before she could control it, as if someone else had taken over her body. She scrambled away, knocking over one of the folding chairs she had against the wall. Her hip hit the corner of her desk, but the pain didn't penetrate.

"Get out, get out!" Tears clouded her vision, but she grabbed the first thing she saw—the plant in the ceramic pot—and threw it at his head. Max dodged and got to his feet, but he didn't try to stop the storm brewing inside of her. The look of sympathy on his face only made the tears fall faster. God, she never cried. Not when she'd been shuffled from one foster home to the next and not when a bullet had pierced her flesh.

The door to her office opened and worried faces peeked in.

"Get out," Max said, and they closed the door with a snap.

Blood trickled from the corner of his mouth,

Excerpt of Concerto of Crows and Cowards

but he was still and silent, letting her rage around him until there was nothing left inside of her but despair. Her breath heaved in and out of her lungs and she let her arms hang down at her side as a sudden weakness seemed to overtake her. Her head dropped down and a chill settled over her skin, making her shiver uncontrollably.

"I want to see him," she said, her voice breaking. "I need to see him."

"Oh, baby," Max said, coming toward her. She let him gather her close, so her head rested on his shoulder. He was grieving too. She could feel the fine tremors coursing through his body. Max and Donovan had been close—as close as most brothers. "You know I can't do that."

"Don't play games with me, Max. I don't care about the red tape or expense reports. I want his body brought back here. I need to see him."

His arms wrapped tight around her and he buried his head against her shoulder. She felt the heat of his tears against her neck, and she tightened her own hold around him, trying to comfort the both of them.

"I can't, Jade." He paused for a few seconds. "There's nothing left of him to bring home."

Something broke inside of her—an agony that started in her womb and ripped and clawed its way through her body. She would have doubled over if Max hadn't been holding her upright. Liquid rushed between her thighs and the coppery scent of blood filled the air.

She tried to scream, but the pain had taken control of her body, rendering her useless.

"Jade!" Max cried out, catching her as her knees gave out and she crumpled to the floor.

She'd lived through unspeakable tragedy in her life—the death of her parents when she was a child, the loss of friends she'd worked and served with, wounds, betrayal, and the loss of her husband—a man she'd loved with everything she'd had to give. But she'd never wanted to die before—not until she lost the only piece of Donovan she had left—the child she'd already imagined to have Donovan's wide grin and her green eyes.

Now there was nothing but blackness as the pain lessened and a cold numbness filled her body. In the back of her mind she thought she heard Max yelling something, calling her name, but she ignored it and embraced the cold. A smile touched her lips when she saw Donovan's face— one last time.

Gabe Brennan is mentioned several times in the Dynamis Security Series as one of the original team members, also known as Ghost. Check out his story in The Lies We Tell. Now available at all retailers!

By her calculations, Grace Meredith had exactly five and a half seconds to take out six targets before an alarm sounded. She had a round in the chamber and five in the magazine of her M40A5. Piece of cake.

She ignored the mosquitoes the size of hummingbirds searching for exposed flesh, and she disregarded the sweat that dripped steadily down her spine as she looked through the scope of her rifle. The temperature was in the mid-nineties, but the canopy of trees that blanketed the area held the heat in like an oven and slowly baked anyone who didn't have shelter with a running AC. Her body and mind were disciplined, so the discomforts barely registered.

Colombia wasn't known for its gentle climate. Or gentle anything for that matter. Gemino Vasquez was Colombia's baddest arms dealer, and lately his biggest client had been North Korea. But Vasquez had something Grace wanted very badly. Something that would bring in a big, fat paycheck from the South Korean government.

She shifted slightly, and the bark of the large tree branch she'd lain on for the last four hours ground against her stomach. But her focus was absolute. Not even the hundred-and-fifty-foot drop to the ground could distract her.

The orange sun blazed just over the tops of the trees, but it would disappear completely in another twenty minutes. By the time it was gone, she'd have the flash drive in hand and already be across the border to Venezuela.

Grace did one final check of all her equipment and took a deep, steadying breath, slowing her heartbeat so her pulse would be in time with-b each shot. She'd hit the sentry at the top of the Vasquez compound first and then take the rest in order from left to right. She pushed her feet against the tree for balance. The clock ticked in the background of her mind as she put the slightest amount of pressure on the trigger.

"One," she whispered. She didn't wait to watch him fall but moved to the next target. Five seconds until the report from her rifle reached their ears. Five seconds for five more kills.

Two…
Three…

Four…
Five…
Six…

Grace didn't stop to check the accuracy of her shots. She never missed a target. She hung her rifle on a tree branch, already missing the feel of it in her hands. Time was of the essence now, and she couldn't afford to be burdened with too much equipment—she'd have to leave it behind. The new guards would be driving up soon for the shift change, and she had to be long gone by then.

She unzipped her supply pack, pulling out a lightweight pipe no longer than her forearm. It looked completely worthless at first glance. In reality, it was a military prototype she'd borrowed from her former life. She hit the button on each end of the pipe and it expanded in length until it was almost as tall as she was, and then she hit the button in the center and waited as wings made out of a synthetic material unfurled to complete the hang glider.

"No time like the present," she said, swallowing as she perched on the edge of the tree and looked out across the jungle. She had a straight shot into the compound, but any shift in wind would have her hurtling into trees. Falling to her death wouldn't bring her the money she needed, so she had no choice but to take a leap of faith. Literally.

Fifteen minutes until all hell breaks loose.

Grace grasped the bar and jumped. The bottom dropped out of her stomach as she free-fell for just a brief moment, and then the air caught beneath the wings and she soared through the treetops like a phantom. It took all her strength and concentration to keep the glider on a straight path to the compound roof, and when her feet touched the ground her muscles were fatigued and her skin coated with perspiration.

She hit another button on the long metal tube and the glider folded itself back up until it was small enough to fit back in her pack.

The body of the first sentry she'd shot lay face down in the greenish-blue water of the swimming pool. A hazy cloud of blood ballooned from under him, and his arms and legs floated like waving ribbons.

Her eyes and ears were alert, but all that greeted her was growing darkness and silence. Even the animals and birds in the jungle knew something bad was about to go down.

Grace unhooked the harness and pulled her SIG from a thigh holster. She stood silently next to

Excerpt of The Lies We Tell

the gray door that led from the roof down a set of stairs to the main floors of the house. Two heartbeats passed before she opened the door and slipped inside. It was quiet, but that wasn't unusual at this time of the day according to her intel—six sentries on duty surrounding the compound, only two guarding Vasquez's private suite of rooms.

Vasquez's stupidity only made her job easier.

Grace walked silently down the thickly carpeted hallway as if she weren't about to steal the schematics for a new superweapon—a weapon that used state-of-the-art laser technology—and sell it to another country. But the closer she got to Vasquez, the more her spine tingled in awareness that something was wrong. That tingle had saved her life more than once, and she never ignored it. The hallway opened up into a landing just as she reached Vasquez's private rooms. Weak light filtered through the windows and cast rainbows as it pierced the glass chandelier that hung overhead.

She saw firsthand exactly why her spine was tingling.

Both sentries were slumped against each other—a dead man's embrace—one with a broken neck and the other with a hunting knife in his carotid. Efficient work considering the size of the sentries.

She pushed the bodies out of her way with her foot and eased the door open, her trigger finger at the ready on her SIG. All that mattered was the flash drive. If she didn't produce it, then she didn't get paid.

She crept into the room. The smells of new death were thick and cloying in the heat, and she could taste the fresh blood in the back of her throat with every breath she took. Dust motes danced in the air, and long shadows were cast in the fading sunlight.

Grace waited for her eyes to adjust and listened for sounds of footsteps, but all she heard was the gentle whir of the wicker fans that rotated slowly on the ceiling. She moved silently, staying close to the wall as she checked his suite.

Vasquez's bedroom was bigger than her whole apartment—the furniture oversized and ornate, the colors garishly red. He was set up for sex. The interesting kind of sex by the looks of things. Restraints and various whips and other tools lined one whole wall, and torn condom packages littered the floor. It looked like Vasquez had a busy day. Too bad his afternoon hadn't turned out so hot.

Excerpt of The Lies We Tell

Gemino Vasquez's body lay spread-eagle on his bed. He was naked, and his eyes were open and unseeing. Two shots to the center of the forehead screamed of a professional hit. He hadn't been dead long. She couldn't stop the bitter disappointment when she saw the flash drive was gone from the chain on his right wrist.

"Hell," she whispered and moved to check the covers of his bed, just to make sure it hadn't come off in the struggle. But she knew in her heart it was long gone. Professionals didn't leave loose ends behind. And this was definitely professional. What ticked her off even more was that whoever did it managed to sneak in right under her nose. He had to have known she was watching through her scope and snuck in through the one blind spot she had at the back of the compound.

The stir of air behind her was the only warning she had before an arm locked around her throat.

"Looking for this?" a deep voice whispered in her ear. He held the flash drive in front of her face.

He pressed close against her back and squeezed his arm tighter around her throat so she had to breathe shallowly through her nose. Grace winced as he pressed his fingers against the pressure points of her wrist, and her pistol fell uselessly to the floor with a dull thunk.

Fear never had a chance to take hold. It was anger that drove Grace. Anger that had kept her alive the last couple of years. And she knew how to wield it. She threw her head back and aimed her heel at his knee simultaneously. He dodged her blows as if he'd been expecting them, but the distraction was enough for him to loosen his grip. She swept her leg and brought him to his knees, reaching down for the knife in her boot. The blade gleamed once in the fading sunlight just before it was knocked out of her hand and across the room.

He outweighed her by close to eighty pounds, and he had a good eight inches on her in height. They grappled and rolled, each one blocking the other's strikes with only seconds to spare. It was a well-choreographed dance.

A familiar dance.

The surprise of recognition took her off guard, and she looked up into laughing blue eyes framed by thick, dark lashes she'd always been jealous of. She had time to register that he'd let his hair grow—a shaggy mane of ink black that curled just over his ears and collar, and a face that was covered in a short, stubbled beard—just before her legs went out from under her. She hit the carpet with a thud. A hard body pressed her into the floor, and he held her wrists captive above her head.

"Hello, darling." His breath whispered against her skin. "You've been practicing. Who's your new sparring partner?"

"Gabe," she said. "What do you want?" She bucked beneath him, annoyed at the familiarity of his weight on her.

"I want you, of course." His lips glanced across her cheek to the corner of her mouth, and she sucked in a breath that brought her body even closer to his. After everything he'd done, he was still the only man who could make her feel less than whole when their bodies weren't fused together. She hated him for it. She hated herself for it.

"Go to hell." She struggled against him, but he shifted his weight to hold her down.

"I've been there, thanks." He cupped his hand against her cheek—gently—softly. "You still feel good against me. Stop wiggling and we'll talk. Don't you want to at least hear my offer? Especially since I did your dirty work for you."

She stilled her body and relaxed, hoping he'd get distracted long enough for her to make a move, and she spoke through gritted teeth. "I don't want anything you have to offer. Just give me the flash drive."

"I figure we have exactly four minutes to get out of this place before the new guards show up for the shift change and Armageddon begins. All I'm asking is that you come back with me and hear me out. If you decide to turn me down, then I'll give you the flash drive with no hard feelings, and you can claim your bounty."

Grace stared at him and tried to decide if he was bluffing. "You know I don't trust you."

"Yes, I believe you've told me that before," he said, his gaze hard. "But what I'm offering will pay more than double any of the jobs you've recently taken. Hear me out."

"Fine." She knew her options were limited. "What are we waiting for?"

"Our rendezvous point is on the other side of the border," he said, rolling off of her. She ignored the hand he reached out to help her up. "We've got twenty minutes to get there or we miss our ride."

Grace had no choice but to follow him out of one hell and into another.

About the Author

Liliana Hart is a *New York Times*, *USA Today*, and Publisher's Weekly bestselling author of more than eighty titles. After starting her first novel her freshman year of college, she immediately became addicted to writing and knew she'd found what she was meant to do with her life. She has no idea why she majored in music.

Since publishing in June 2011, Liliana has sold more than ten-million books. All three of her series have made multiple appearances on the New York Times list.

Liliana can almost always be found at her computer writing, hauling five kids to various activities, or spending time with her husband. She calls Texas home.

If you enjoyed reading this book, I would appreciate it if you would help others enjoy this book too.

Recommend it. Please help other readers find this book by recommending it to friends, readers' groups and discussion boards.

Review it. Please tell other readers why you liked this book by reviewing.

Connect with me online:
www.lilianahart.com

Also by Liliana Hart

Laurel Valley

Tribulation Pass

Redemption Road

Midnight Clear

JJ Graves Mystery Series

Dirty Little Secrets

A Dirty Shame

Dirty Rotten Scoundrel

Down and Dirty

Dirty Deeds

Dirty Laundry

Dirty Money

A Dirty Job

Dirty Devil

Playing Dirty

Dirty Martini

Dirty Dozen

Dirty Minds

Dirty Weekend

Dirty Looks

Addison Holmes Mystery Series

Whiskey Rebellion

Whiskey Sour

Whiskey For Breakfast

Whiskey, You're The Devil

Whiskey on the Rocks

Whiskey Tango Foxtrot

Whiskey and Gunpowder

Whiskey Lullaby

The Scarlet Chronicles

Bouncing Betty

Hand Grenade Helen

Front Line Francis

The Harley and Davidson Mystery Series

The Farmer's Slaughter

A Tisket a Casket

I Saw Mommy Killing Santa Claus

Get Your Murder Running

Deceased and Desist

Malice in Wonderland

Tequila Mockingbird

Gone With the Sin

Grime and Punishment

Blazing Rattles

A Salt and Battery

Curl Up and Dye

First Comes Death Then Comes Marriage

Box Set 1

Box Set 2

Box Set 3

The Gravediggers

The Darkest Corner

Gone to Dust

Say No More

Printed in Great Britain
by Amazon